STARLIGHT SEDUCTION

A Steamy Professor Romantic Comedy, featuring the bonus
short story No Guts, No Gasms

LARISSA LYNX

Starlight Seduction is dedicated to Sharon and DJ, two uniquely wonderful women who introduced me to the magical world we live in and enriching friendships beyond typical boundaries.

At Literary Madness, we strive to create a book free of typos. If you notice anything amiss, we're happy to fix it. litmadness@yahoo.com

Contemporaries by Larissa Lynx

POWER PLAYERS HOCKEY series

*My Two-Stud Stand**

*Her Three Studs**

The Stud Takes a Stand (2022)

**Her Hockey Studs - print version*

SEXY CONTEMPORARY ROMANCE

Renegade Kisses

Starlight Seduction

SHORT 'N' SUPER STEAMY

A Heart for Adam...& Rick!

Braving Donovan's

No Guts, No 'Gasms

Historicals by Larissa Lyons

ROARING ROGUES REGENCY SHIFTERS

Ensnared by Innocence

Deceived by Desire (2022)

Tamed by Temptation (TBA)

MISTRESS IN THE MAKING series (Complete)

Seductive Silence

Lusty Letters

Daring Declarations

FUN & SEXY REGENCY ROMANCE

Lady Scandal

A SWEETLY SPICY REGENCY

Miss Isabella Thaws a Frosty Lord

Contents

Author's Note   9

Starlight Seduction

1. Astrology   15
2. Astronomy   35
3. Fairy   51
4. Magic   71
5. Make-Believe   95
6. Kismet   117

No Guts, No Gasms

About No Guts, No Gasms   135
1. The Sexy Bad Boy   139
2. Good Girl Gone Brave   151

A Free Story & More Fun Books!   167
About Larissa   177

Author's Note

In the mid-2000s my first *completed** story won a contest sponsored by Liquid Silver Publishing. That 16,000 word story, *Written in the Stars*, went on to become the longer *Sex and Solar Flares*, released by Ellora's Cave.

Light editing and a fresh proofread were given for this—the last edition, *Starlight Seduction*. During the initial writing of this story and in the years since, my absolute favorite scene remains the shipboard star party. I hope you enjoy it as much as Aurora and Charlie. Happy reading!

*A big deal because while I'm great at starting things, *finishing* sometimes presents a challenge—one I'm working on!

Starlight Seduction

Let all the number of the stars give light to thy fair way!

—William Shakespeare, *Antony and Cleopatra*

ONE

Astrology

ASTROLOGY – n., *The—to some, dubious—science that studies how the location and rotation of stellar and planetary bodies affect the workings of our day-to-day lives; one's date of birth frequently plays a significant role in chart calculations and analysis.*

FINAL ASSIGNMENT.

Goal: Bind the goat.

Reward for Success: Choice of next assignment.

Penalty for Failure: Doomed to banishment upon—

UPON...WHAT?

Aurora had yet to finish skimming the cryptic missive before Tragar snapped his stubby green fingers, disintegrating the parchment.

"What does—" Before she finished the sentence, she'd vanished. Become nothing more than a wisp on a whirlwind.

In a kaleidoscope of color Aurora hurtled through space, zipping past nebulas...star clusters...the Dog Star Sirius in Canis Major...even that shiny thing labeled *Voyager*. Ah, she must be headed to Earth. Early-to-mid twenty-first century or thereabouts if she wasn't mistaken.

How wondrous. After studying the planet and its cultures, she'd always longed to visit. How long might she—

Umpf! Aurora's feet slammed onto the ground, the landing ricocheting straight up her spine like a jolt from Mushroom Moonshine, one of her sister's naughty specialties.

Before her tottering legs found their balance or her eyes adjusted to the bright sun shining overhead, a strange, prickling heat unlike anything she'd ever experienced flowed from her fingertips straight up her arm.

She looked at her hand, blinking rapidly, trying to focus, but her hair had tangled and twisted during the interstellar voyage. Through the unruly strands, she saw her fingers wrapped tightly around tweed-covered muscle. Smoldering muscle that flexed beneath her tight grip. At the realization of how intimately close she was to a stranger, heat spiraled through her body.

"Whoa there." A deep, husky voice washed over

her, full of nuance beyond the brief syllables. "You all right?"

Aurora glanced up—way up—under the cover of her hair.

Sunspots and solar flares! Talk about a magnificent male specimen. Bigger than any she'd seen up close, he commanded every ounce of her attention.

"Pardon me," he continued in tones that bathed her ears with their masculine timbre, "I didn't see you there. Didn't mean to bump into you."

So *not* the case, given how she'd crashed into him.

She couldn't help but compare him to the slender, oft effeminate males back home. Males who usually flitted around naked and completely exposed. Not only was his brawny size their exact opposite, this man wore clothing—and loads of it. Dark, heavy garments layered upon his body, the fabrics full of texture and substance. She longed to trace the material with her fingers almost as much as she longed to take it off. Her fingers clenched around his forearm, body blazed at the unbidden thought.

His forearm flexed beneath her grip.

Self-consciously, she released her hold, fingers still burning from the contact.

Around them, the air buzzed with activity, hummed with the conversation from a myriad humans. Too many to count. But only one held her in thrall. Captivated and consumed.

The splendid example of manhood before her.

Did all human specimens project such high temperatures? The males on her homeworld never caused these feelings. This *heat.*

"Ma'am?" He placed strong fingers on her shoulder and rocked her universe again. "Sure you're all right?"

Hiding her unexpected reaction to him, she nodded absently and bent to unwrap the dress that had wound around her legs, and stalling for time. Toadstools and tulips, this wasn't like her. Where was her composure? Her usual disinterest in males? Completing her studies taking priority, of course.

"Is this your first cruise?" he asked in his resonant, deep tones that rumbled through her like thunder over a mountainscape.

Cruise? Cruise!

Maggots and moonspiders! That meant *ocean.*

Tragar could have told her that, tricky troll. Was he trying to test her mettle along with her mind?

Childhood fears of dark depths and nearly drowning threatened to swamp— But wait...

The stranger's presence proved a distraction from her murky thoughts. Who could wallow in bad memories when tempting warmth from such an alluring presence hovered nearby?

Still messing with her skirt, she made a sound of agreement. "Mmmmm."

"First trip to Hawaii?"

Aurora was more comfortable observing humans from afar. Conversing so soon upon landing was proving quite the conundrum, English being her seventh language and all. And studied mainly from old printed texts, which she preferred to electronic versions, no matter how "backwater" her siblings claimed it made her. Or was that "backwoods"?

Moonbeams and morning glories, she hated being at a loss! The right words would come to her, she was sure, *if* she could just quit sizzling from his unexpected presence.

The man's focused attention unnerved her, even as she yearned for it. Reveled in it. Instincts long ignored and muscles long unused began clamoring for attention. She glanced at his face.

He was staring at her legs. *Oooo*, there went her temperature, spiking again. What had he asked her? Oh Hawaii. Hawaii?

She ordered her sluggish brain to compute. Data. Facts. Where were they?

She'd studied enough, had a keen fascination with Earthlings and humans that mystified her troll teachers, so she *should* know. Why couldn't she remember—

And then like magic, there it was, the information she sought:

Hawaii. Polynesian culture. Fiftieth state to join the United States in 1959. Hula dancers, Don Ho and "Tiny Bubbles". Known as a tropical paradise, a popular vacation spot luring visitors from across the planet.

As other tidbits flew into her brain, she straightened and looked at him through her long bangs. "Aye, 'tis my first visit." No, that didn't sound quite right. Too archaic. "Umm, *yeah*."

"Mine too. First vacation in years. Well, if you call a job interview vacation," he explained with a smile that carved twin dimples in his rugged face, giving the first hint of boyish charm to an otherwise masculine countenance that drew her mightily.

Firm, square jaw, covered with just a few hours' worth of stubble, trim sideburns and stylish sunglasses that put her in mind of one of the movie star celebrities her sister Trixie liked to moon over.

She wanted to touch his hair. Short and light, the color of sunshine, it spiked from his scalp, just begging her to run her fingers through it. Was it as warm as it looked? What about his face? His chest? Were they hot too? And what was she doing obsessing over either when she should be contemplating her studies and perplexing final assignment for this cycle? *Bind the goat?* What *on earth* did that mean?

"I have an appointment at the observatory on Mauna Kea to see about a job. Charles Morigan, from Arizona." He held out his hand.

It was big too, just like the man. She could feel the heat emanating from his fingers.

Directly behind her, a loud noise blared from a speaker. The shrill sound careened between her ears and she winced. Heart in her throat, stomach somewhere around her toes, Aurora tried to calm her reaction and appear unaffected.

Before she had time to assume a relaxed pose, the man cocked his head toward an entrance that led to a narrow walkway. "Oh, they just announced M through P. Guess I'm supposed to board now. Well... ahem." He slowly retracted his hand and curved it into a fist. "Perhaps I'll see you around."

The moment he walked off, she leaned forward into the space he'd vacated and inhaled.

Spicy...strong...sexy.

Arousing.

How could a man smell strong? Strong wasn't a scent! Yet his lingered—

Bind the goat. The goat.

The puzzling instructions intruded in her mind as her eyes followed the man's progress.

She *really* wanted to touch his hair.

MAYBE THE FISH WAS BAD.

The queasy feeling in his gut had started earlier and had grown steadily worse through dinner. He gave the uneaten fish on his plate a dirty look, wishing he'd smuggled his faithful feline on board. Ol' cactus-head would've taken a single sniff and turned up his nose, giving Charles advance warning.

Damn! Just what he needed to start off the first real semi-vacation he'd taken in six years—food poisoning. While Prickly Pear was home dining on caviar and canned kitty goodness—Charles had stocked up to ease his guilt over being gone for so long.

His stomach rolled.

Double damn, this vacation was going to the dogs.

"Have you sailed on the *Seaward Splendor* before, Mr. Morigan?"

At the sound of his name, he looked up from his plate, determined to ignore the churning sensations.

One of the elderly women seated across the large circular table smiled at him, her look expectant. He thought her name was Hazel. Or maybe Mabel. Before he could answer, one of the matching women flanking her chided, "Harriet, it's *Professor* Morigan. Did you forget, dear?"

Harriet. Now he remembered. When he'd been seated at his assigned table and seen the three nearly identical octogenarians, he'd done a double take then a triple take. Harriet was the most outspoken, her bright orange hair matched by the god-awful orange lipstick she'd all but chewed off the past half-hour.

"Charles is fine," he told them. Actually, it was *Doctor* Morigan but he didn't want to correct them and come across as pretentious. This trip was supposed to be relaxing, casual...a far cry from his usual twelve-plus-hour workdays. "And no, ma'am.

It's my first time out to sea in something other than a fishing boat."

Which he'd enjoyed—and never once gotten seasick.

Damn fish.

"It's our fourteenth cruise." Blue-haired Hazel-Mabel told him with pride, waving her napkin in front of her like a flag. "Worth celebrating, I do declare! Which is why I wanted to treat tonight," she added with a little hiccup, indicating her fondness for the wine that'd been shared among everyone occupying their table.

"I think you're mistaken, sister. I do believe this is number fifteen," Harriet corrected. She reached into her purse and pulled out a tube of lipstick, heaven help the old dear.

"Well, I think *you're* confused, Harry. Don't you remember, the Mediterranean was twelfth and then we did Alaska the second time, then we sailed..."

The sisters continued to debate amid themselves, leaving him free to contemplate his fish. Or not.

He'd rather think about the woman on the dock this morning. Damn. There went his stomach again. One moment he'd been standing in line, reading over the ship's itinerary. The next, a strong breeze blew past him and he felt a small hand clamped around his arm. From his first glance at the woman's lithe body and long, thick hair, he wanted a lot more than her hand clamped around him.

Visions of her nude and riding him like some modern-day Lady Godiva with his brawny body her steed had plagued him ever since. So easily could he picture her petite frame writhing atop him, her fascinating, mahogany hair streaming down, ensnaring them both...

Uncharacteristic, as Charles had left his imagination in elementary school.

A man of science and notable scholastic achievement, his mother would intone on the rare occasions he'd dared read a friend's book full of fairy tales or wizards or any manner of forbidden make-believe, *doesn't waste time with his head in the clouds.* The admonishment was usually followed by something similar to *Now go practice spelling the elements, dear. Your father expects you to know the rest of the periodic table by this weekend. Or Recite pi out to the hundredth digit.*

Blah, blah. His scholarly parents had tried to suck all the fun and wonder right out of his childhood.

The hum of the engines changed as they picked up speed, breaking Charles from the past. A place he seldom visited these days, both of his multiple Ph.D.-holding parents no longer having any hold over him. Not since he'd moved half a country away from their naysaying and negativity.

He *liked* having his head in the clouds, dammit. Liked more the thought of taking his fellow, long-haired, soft-spoken passenger there with him.

Idly, he watched the liquid in his wineglass shimmy with the ship's motion. Now that they were away from port and in open waters, he'd expected the movement of the huge ship to increase, anticipating something along the lines of giant *whumping ka-thumps* as it sliced through the oceanic swells. But instead, the constant, low-grade vibration was easy to acclimate to. Reminding him of those cheap motel beds he'd loved playing on as a kid—whenever he could escape for the weekend with a friend. The ones that shimmied for a quarter.

He'd tried to engage the woman in conversation, but her monosyllabic replies hadn't been encouraging. Too bad...she was one female he'd sure like to get on a bed, vibrating or otherwise.

As if conjured by his thoughts, she entered the cavernous dining room, stopping abruptly when she saw the packed tables. Charles barely restrained the urge to jump up and shout, "Here! There's an empty chair right here!"

EARLIER THAT DAY, relieved when the proper identification and Earth-based currencies came instantly to hand as they were requested, Aurora had boarded the large vessel and found her designated cabin. Though compact, the room was light and airy and surprisingly smelled of magnolia blossoms, her favorite scent.

Credit cards, passport, magnolia-scented cabins! The things Tragar could arrange from halfway across the galaxy. Astonishing.

She'd removed the slim purse that'd been strapped over her shoulder when she'd landed, complete with everything she'd needed to pass for a card-carrying human. Dropping it on the bed next to a handsome floral bag bearing a tag with her name on it, she nearly lit up like a glowworm. Her first overnight assignment on Earth! She couldn't wait to begin exploring in the guise of completing her task.

Static sounded from overhead then a clipped voice came from her ceiling. "As your captain, I'd like to welcome everyone aboard. Starting tomorrow morning, room service will be available. Tonight's formal dinner is in the main hall, seating at seven and nine p.m., though dress codes are relaxed our first night out. Anytime you prefer something more casual, we have a number of eateries located throughout the ship. And don't forget to indulge in a swirl cone! Seventeen years captaining ships and I still tip my hat to those automatic ice cream machines. Right. Heh-heh. A glare from my first mate reminds me to get back to business. Before we leave San Diego and the States, everyone must present themselves on deck for our required safety lesson. Keep your ears tuned. In approximately five minutes, the signal for our safety drill will sound and we'll all practice the routine. I expect smooth sailing but better safe than sorry, eh?"

While waiting for the safety alarm, Aurora emptied the packed bag and explored her clothing options, dismayed to discover her illustrious instructor hadn't included a single pair of human shoes. No strappy sandals, no heavy combat boots. No thick, fuzzy socks either.

Aurora waved her hand. Nothing happened. She hadn't really expected it to, not this soon. All right then, no choice but to go barefoot.

Fortunately a number of her favorite swirly dresses were tucked neatly inside with nary a wrinkle. If she had to wear clothes, her gossamer dresses were the next best thing to being naked. Searching for the missive that'd disappeared from her grasp earlier, she found her dining room table number and scheduled time, but that was it. Nothing else.

Then the wretched buzzer blasted and she escaped outside.

Aurora suffered through the crowded safety lesson the best she could, listening to the speech patterns of those sardined—an expression a fellow passenger had used—around her. Though she wanted to fit in and sound "hip", those goals took a seat behind simply giving her body time to acclimate to Earth's mass and atmosphere.

For one used to flying solo, or only with her favorite unicorn for company, her acute senses were undergoing massive overload from being in such close proximity with so many humans.

But soon the vessel was sailing on the high seas.

Instead of floating through the air—which had become commonplace after she earned her wings —she was floating on the ocean. Despite the anxiety storming her insides, she couldn't help but be exhilarated. Flowers and fireflies, this was exciting.

Thrilled to her bare toes, determined to ignore the growing flood of emotions she sensed from the human passengers, Aurora tackled her latest assignment—when all she really wanted to do was search for a glimpse of sunny-haired Charles Morigan from Arizona.

But her studious side prevailed and she sincerely looked for the goat.

And looked for the goat.

And looked...for...the...goat.

It was useless. Giving the ocean-side railings a wide—very wide—berth, she searched every available inch of the ship yet came up empty. When she tried to check the cargo hold, a crewman barred the entrance. She refused to leave until he promised there wasn't a goat hiding behind the door. Glaring at her as though he thought *she* needed to be tied up, he assured her the ship was goat free, that nary a goat ever traveled on the *Seaward Splendor*. Even went so far as to claim the head chef never served *cabrito*.

It took Aurora a good thirty seconds to recall that *cabrito* was the Spanish word for barbecued goat. Blech! Poison and pumpernickel, but that was unappealing, fairies being staunch vegetarians and all.

Thoroughly frustrated, she nevertheless considered the bright side. She'd explored the ship and in the process had discovered a secluded area that looked out over the ocean. Though she hadn't braved nearing the rail, the late afternoon sun glinting off the ship's wake had reminded her of the man's hair, all gold and enticing. Thoughts of him made her throat go dry. Confirming no one was around, she waved one hand and held out the other, expecting a full glass of crisp, refreshing water to appear.

It didn't.

Oh asteroids and azaleas, she *still* didn't have any magic. The solar flares must be really strong today if her magic hadn't caught up with her yet.

Disillusioned, Aurora returned to her cabin and flopped on the bed. How could she tie up the dad-blamed goat if she couldn't find it? Used to quick success, the unfamiliar fog of pending failure weighed on her mind. Even the inviting cabin didn't lift her spirits.

Her stomach growled, reminding her of the distance she'd traveled without nourishment. If she couldn't summon something on her own, she'd have to eat with the humans. Afterward, she'd enjoy a warm shower then rest. She'd look for the darn goat again tomorrow.

While she retrieved an outfit from her bag,

Aurora wondered when Tragar would call her back. *If* he called her back. She hadn't failed an assignment before and didn't know how long she'd be here. Pity—she wouldn't mind having some time to look for the man with the dark clothes and sunshine hair. *Mr. Charles Morigan,* of the steel-strong arms and sexy scent. *Charlie.*

Distracted by her thoughts, the elegant braid she attempted to pull her hair into was nothing more than a snarled mess, which she promptly blamed on Tragar. His instructions for this latest assignment didn't make any sense. Stupid troll. She'd like to give him a wart on the end of his nose, one to match the mole already there. But that wouldn't exactly endear Aurora to her current instructor.

Thanks to Tragar's terrible tutelage, her perfect assignment record seemed doomed, and she was dragging when she left her cabin.

A headache pounded between her eyes. If she hadn't been so hungry, she would've skipped supper. How could she have known being around humans would be such a strain? Fairies were intuitive, Aurora more so than many. And though the emotions of the many passengers were for the most part positive and upbeat, suffering such a barrage of new impressions assaulted her sensitive receptors.

Even after her ship-wide search for *el cabrito* which should have familiarized her with the vessel, she made several wrong turns on the way to dinner. Finally she gave up and followed her nose, easily sniffing out the scents of food and humans once she lowered her guard.

By the time she located the main dining room, everyone was seated. Conversation and laughter clashed with the cacophony of people eating. Her sensitive ears heard it all, increasing the pressure in her head. Standing just inside the door, drained and despondent from the long day, she didn't see an empty chair anywhere. Nor was anyone occupying the podium off to the side.

So she waited. Yet the longer she stood there, the more she noticed people staring at her. Oh seeds and weeds, how she hated being the center of attention. Maybe she should skip supper after all? A protest rumbled from her stomach.

Weary and out of sorts, Aurora considered retreating—her belly could just suffer. Just then an officious man scurried over. After asking her table number and *tsking* over how very late she was, how hungry she must be, he hurriedly escorted her through the dining room.

When they neared their destination, he raised his arms and clapped, summoning a waiter, the sound causing an unwelcome tremor to thunder through her head. But that was forgotten the moment they reached the table because everything faded into oblivion. Her exhaustion...the goat...even her headache.

He was here! Sitting at this very table! The man with the sunny hair. *Charlie.*

Energy and excitement thrummed through Aurora. When she approached the empty seat, he stood and pulled out her chair. Stars and satellites, he was big.

Shivers danced over her skin as she sensed his nearness along her entire left side.

Before she even sat down, the newly arrived waiter thrust a menu in front of her, rattling off options and recommendations, worried the kitchen was about to close for the night.

She was expected to make a decision? To actually possess the mental ability to comprehend and choose from among the gourmet human options? To *read* English? Now? When her entire world was taken up by the man at her side? *Pfft!* Aurora just pointed and handed the menu back, so hungry she could eat a harpy.

Charlie was so close. If she inhaled deeply enough, they'd touch. The thought made her lightheaded.

She practically wilted into her chair, giddiness—and no doubt hunger—stealing her strength. Charlie's breath was warm on the back of her neck when he pushed in her chair and she nearly went through the ceiling in response.

Several other people voiced their hellos and welcomes, and Aurora smiled and nodded, pretending to understand while inside she was awhirl with thoughts and possibilities. When the waiter brought her food a moment later, she mindlessly ate, considering her options.

Maybe the goat *hadn't* made it on board the ship. She *had* looked on all twelve decks. Twice. If Tragar couldn't see fit to give her better instructions, then she couldn't be blamed for not completing this assignment. At least that sounded like something her sister Trixie would say.

"Wine, miss?" Another waiter interrupted her musings. "It's already paid for by one of your table mates."

"Aye, thank you."

"Red or white? They're both excellent, if I may be so bold."

More decisions? Couldn't these overly obsequious humans tell her mind was otherwise occupied? Striving for a polite and proper response, Aurora pasted on a smile. "I will be agog with either."

She nodded absently at whatever he replied, no longer paying any attention as pale liquid splashed into her wineglass. Staring deeply into the gently bubbling brew, she ate faster, her mind brimming with ideas.

Goats...assignments...alcohol...Charlie. Big, sexy Charlie...

TWO

Astronomy

ASTRONOMY – n., *The science that studies celestial bodies, including their classification, distance from Earth, chemical composition, probable origination and potential destruction.*

"ISN'T THAT RIGHT, PROFESSOR MORIGAN?"

"Huh?" he mumbled, his eyes glued to the woman standing by the dining room's entrance. When the maître d' began escorting her toward the table where Charles sat, his whole body jerked to attention like a Mexican jumping bean at a *frijoles fiesta.*

The woman practically floated as she made her way past the other diners. She wore another long dress, this one so sheer and filmy he swore he could see the dark shadow of her nipples. Maybe he could sneak a glance down her front, see them in full view?

The thought was so unlike him, he slapped a hand to his forehead. Trying to knock some sense in?

"Professor, did I hear you say you studied the stars?" The question came from across the table. "Professor?"

All his attention on the woman, he responded distractedly. "Uh, yes. I...I'm...an astron...o..."

His words trailed off when the maître d' led the woman directly to the chair next to his. Charles rushed to his feet and pulled it out. She gracefully sank onto it, giving him a shy nod of thanks. Their waiter promised he'd bring her food right out when she indicated her choice. Charles watched as she folded her napkin in her lap, took a sip of water and looked anywhere but at him.

He itched to touch the delicate fabric of her dress. The symphony of colors swirling around her sent his senses spinning. The muscles in his throat tightened. He loosened his tie and sat down.

Why wouldn't she look at him?

He couldn't remember a time he'd been this attracted to a woman, when garnering her attention mattered more. Work and research occupied so much of his life that he'd had little interest in fostering a relationship.

The only son of two highly accomplished physicists in their mid-forties by the time he made an unexpected—and unwelcome, he couldn't help but surmise—appearance, nothing Charles ever did was good enough for their exalted standards.

His first-place finish in the school science fair? Not acceptable because he came in *third* at district. Full college scholarship to the Caltech Astronomy Department at sixteen? Not laud-worthy because they'd been admitted at fourteen. To Princeton.

Which wasn't to say he was a total geek. Far from it.

He played on a paintball league—or had in his twenties.

He had a Facebook page—with nearly 400 friends last count. Or was it followers? One of his students had made it for him several years ago when he'd started teaching the occasional class at the local university. He was constantly being poked and prodded for not checking in more. But after spending most of his days and many of his nights chained to a computer when he wasn't behind a lecture podium, could he be blamed for not wanting to tie himself to it after-hours?

At thirty-seven and after one failed engagement —he'd broken things off when the accomplished mathematics professor he'd dated for two years started reminding him of his *mother*—Charles wanted change. Change in a big way.

Wasn't sure whether he'd find it in Hawaii, but he was hoping...

Had—to his embarrassment—even wished upon Deneb, the brightest star in the sky last night. Well, brightest star he could see, cloud cover obstructing his view of Altair and Vega. Him—a man holding advanced degrees in Astrophysics and Astronomy, wishing on stars. *Thhbbb*! Stupid nonsense, he knew. Which didn't explain why he'd done it.

Thinking about his forlorn past and somewhat lonely present soured his stomach all over again. Swinging his attention from self-recrimination to—dare he think it?—*hope*, he glanced longingly at the woman next to him. Too easily could he envision her sitting front and center in his life. Better yet, front and centered *on his lap*.

Charles shifted, trying to relieve the pressure.

Well, shit. He hadn't dated in so long he'd lost any semblance of self-control as well as his finesse. Tomorrow at dinner, he'd attempt talking to her again. By the end of this long cruise, maybe they'd actually engage in a real conversation. Oh joy. Too bad he wanted a lot more than conversation...

He moved the fish around on his plate and tried to focus on the chatter buzzing around him.

"See, Harriet, I told you the professor here was an astrologer."

Sitting beside him in her flowing dress, the woman was so graceful and fresh, like a field of wildflowers. The image, in stark contrast to the sterile science lab where he worked on his non-teaching days analyzing data from telescope observations, imprinted itself on his brain.

"I am thrilled to hear that! Maybe he'll do a reading for us. My last astrologer had to retire. Shut down by the IRS for nonpayment of taxes and all. It's been ages since I've gotten a good reading."

"I've wanted to do that for years, I declare! Get a personal reading. I read my horoscope every morning, you know, but I never—"

"Leave the man alone, Mabel, Harry. He's on vacation." A loud thump of a cane accompanied this announcement.

He really wanted to talk to the fey beauty, but she hadn't returned his conversational gambits earlier and she was doing her best to ignore him now. His back teeth ground, giving vent to his frustration.

"I bet he wouldn't mind. Would you, Professor Morigan?"

"Hmmm?" He was so damn distracted, his brain wasn't paying attention. If he only knew why she seemed uncomfortable around him. Maybe she was just shy, but he was a little afraid to try again. What if she flat wasn't interested?

Try! Try again! his cock urged, uncaring of the possible blow to his ego.

"Would you mind reading the stars for us, Professor? Tonight?"

"Harry, give the man a break." *Thump, thump* went the cane.

"Shhh. Let him answer, Hazel. Professor Morigan?"

"Umm." His mind clouded with want, he attempted to make sense of the words. Stars. Tonight. Oh, they must want him to give a constellation tour, something he did on a monthly basis back home as part of his ongoing educational outreach for the community. "Yeah." His tongue was thick in his mouth. He loosened his tie even more. "Sure. The stars? I'll be happy to."

He'd be happier if the alluring female wasn't behaving as though looking at him would turn her to stone.

The waiter brought her food and she devoured it with such gusto he wondered if he'd be called upon to perform the Heimlich. Hey, at least that way he'd get to touch her, right?

Why was she acting so skittish around him? Refusing to shake his hand this morning, barely acknowledging him tonight. Women! He didn't understand them a lick. This one more than most.

Just then, the skinny-ass Italian waiter came over to refill everyone's drinks, and she smiled and spoke to the scrawny man. Come to think of it, when the other guy had escorted her to the table—a puny, pipsqueak of a fellow who looked as if he wouldn't know what to do with a woman if she stepped naked into his shower—she'd been smiling shyly and glowing then too.

Damn! Charles had his answer.

It was his size again. At six-foot-four and 210 pounds, he was built more like a linebacker than a scientist and part-time college professor. It wasn't that he clomped around or was clumsy, just that he was, well...big. Solid. Over the years, his size intimidated a lot of women, especially small, delicate ones who didn't know him well. Like the beauty sitting next to him.

Could he help it if he looked more like a beefy boxer than a debonair ladies' man?

He usually wasn't intrigued enough to care.

And he shouldn't care now. So why did he?

After all, he was here for a job interview. He hadn't come on this cruise to get laid.

MIDWAY THROUGH DINNER, Aurora made a decision and reached for her untouched wineglass. In two gulps she drank half the contents.

Alcohol made her horny. Really, really horny—at least it should, according to her sister who was an authority on the subjects of alcohol and men. Liquor also clipped her wings, which wasn't a position any self-respecting fairy wanted to be in. Not that Aurora was a full-fledged fairy. Not yet anyway.

She was a third-cycle apprentice. And at the top of her class—until today. A lonely position, something she usually didn't notice because studying and assignments took up all of her time. Her feminine needs had been sorely neglected.

Needs that Trixie said a human man could take care of. In a big way. Her younger sister had loads of experience with males and she was forever telling Aurora to pay more attention to her body's desires and less to her studies. Ignoring Trixie's outlandish advice had been easy in the past. Before today, Aurora hadn't been around many real men. Certainly no hu-*men*. At the moment though, she'd sure like to be clasped around the one next to her.

As she unthinkingly ate the food on her plate, she watched him under the cover of her hair. She'd studied so many eras on Earth before, in times both preceding and following this one, but never had she found a human male so fascinating. Seeing them through a screen or holo-program hadn't prepared her in the least. Not for how their emotions fairly swamped her receptors; nor how she reacted to *this* particular one.

The sincere tone of his deep voice made her melt. Each time he spoke to the other humans, flutters flew up and down her spine, tantalized her wing lines. She eyed the way his strong hands gently handled the cutlery, the way he carefully held his wineglass. How would he touch her skin? Her breasts...her arse? No, that didn't seem quite right. Hiney? Buttocks? *Butt*? That was it.

At the thought of his bare hands on her butt, her under-used libido jumpstarted, revved and, after half a glass of wine, was raring to go. She'd had sex with male fairies before. It was no big deal. Nothing ever made her wings flutter or her body glow like thoughts of Charlie touching her did.

She tried to think of every way she knew to seduce a man. The list was short. Short as in nonexistent. Trixie would know what to do. Aurora could just hear her sister saying, "Human males are easy. They always want sex. Just ask."

Okay, so maybe this wasn't the simplest task she'd undertaken, but it certainly promised to be one of the most satisfying. Thinking of satisfaction, the muscles between her legs clenched.

Quickly reaching for her water glass—she needed to cool down fast—she accidentally bumped his arm. Ummm. She knew something else she'd like to bump into.

The ship would be at sea for only five nights before arriving in port and she didn't know when Tragar might call her back. Five nights didn't seem nearly enough for the erotic adventures she wanted to indulge in if she had the gumption to go for it.

She did! She wanted it all. *With Charlie.*

Matching actions to intent, Aurora returned her water glass without taking a sip. She picked up her wine and drained it in one motion. When she placed the glass on the table, she deliberately knocked against the man once more.

THE WOMAN next to him nudged his arm yet again. Awareness zinged through his body and landed in his stomach like a supernova.

Steak. He should have skipped the cod and gone for the steak.

"Oops. I beg your pardon," she said in a soft, melodious whisper.

"No harm done," he told her, thinking the third time's a charm. It was the third time their elbows had connected during dinner. And the first time she'd spoken directly to him.

Shy or not, she was one smart lady. She'd ordered the steak. Steak he'd watched her inhale as if she hadn't eaten in a week. Seeing her luscious lips wrapped around her fork and sliding off pieces of meat had spurred all sorts of lurid ideas. He'd like to have her lips wrapped around him, sliding back and forth. His stomach twinged, pulling his mind out of his pants. The warmth from her touch was still zipping down his arm. He swallowed and loosened his tie a bit more. At this rate, it'd be hanging from his neck in no time, the ends trailing down to his waist.

What had made him wear the damn thing? He was on vacation, for God's sake, not standing in front of a hundred college students, lecturing on spectral analysis. Past the strangling sensation, he offered, "Would you like to switch places?"

She glanced at their elbows, barely an inch apart, then nodded. He nearly saw past the long bangs covering her forehead to catch a glimpse of her eyes, but she kept her head ducked, even when she spoke again. "Left-hander's curse, I fear." She laughed, causing the supernova in his stomach to head south. "I'm forever bumping into right-handed people."

It was the most she'd said to him. Progress at last. He wished she wouldn't hide behind her hair. If only he could see her eyes. He yearned to grasp her chin and hold her still, to discover their color, to study her features.

Talk about inexplicable body chemistry. No scientific reasoning here for how very attracted he was to a woman he'd yet to fully view. One he didn't know a thing about.

Charisma.

Animal attraction.

Sex appeal.

She oozed that intangible *something*. Maybe it just oozed between them; maybe it was all in his head. But real or imagined, he felt its force in full sway, his fact-leaning past be damned.

Standing, he pulled back her chair, taking care not to step on her long, shimmery dress. His fingers itched to dive into the thick, dark hair tied in a jumbled knot at her nape. Her head was at the level of his ready-to-party dick and he imagined sinking his hand into her hair and guiding her mouth to him. His grip on the chair tightened. He stood closer, disguising his condition.

Before she could rise and take his seat, one of the triplets hollered out, "Are you two heading off already? But the dessert waiter is just now making his rounds. You can't skip dessert. It's one of the best things about vacation. And what about the stars? I thought you—"

"Harry, dear, leave the young people alone. They probably want to retire early. *Together.*"

Not a bad idea, old girl. Lest the lovely lady think him a lecher, he roused his rusty chivalrous instincts in order to correct Mabel-Hazel's words, as much as he might wish otherwise. "Oh no. We aren't leaving to-geth..."

His sentence stumbled to a halt when he felt the woman shift in her seat and caress the back of his hand. The deliberate touch went straight to his groin. She stood, trailing her fingers across his arm —raising gooseflesh in her wake and his cock in his pants. She looked directly into his eyes.

Purple.

Well, what do you know? Her eyes were purple. Dark lavender. Sparkly plum. Amazing. Freaking amazing. As he studied the amethyst-colored irises, his stomach dipped again. Maybe he wasn't cut out for life on the high seas?

"Does thy wish to?" she whispered. "Leave together? Cleave together and become one flesh?"

Holy shit. Not so shy and innocent after all.

Did he want them to leave together? To *cleave* together? Were there stars in the sky? Did the sun burn hotter than 5,000 degrees Celsius? Was his body so hard and ready that he'd die if he didn't have her?

Hell yes, he wanted to leave with her.

But what was up with that King James-Shakespearian speech of hers? More than that, what was going on with his stomach?

Could it be the woman affecting him this way? Ridiculous. He was a grown man. It had to be the fish.

Didn't it?

Either way, he was screwed. He hoped.

———◦———

"NOT GOOD. NOT." The words escaped past pointy, jagged teeth and evaporated into the ether.

Watching the foolish twit make dopey doe eyes at the human, Tragar scratched his long nose, disgusted. How was he supposed to teach Aurora anything if she wouldn't stay focused on her assignment? And she'd started out the cycle so promising too. "Such a waste. Such."

Third-year apprentices tended to be full of themselves. After mastering the art of flying and pixie dust usage, getting them to pay attention in the classroom practically took a command from Queen Arlene. Aurora had been the brightest ray of sunshine in this year's crop of hopefuls. The young sprite, ignoring the examples of her rebellious siblings, actually came to class, kept her feet on the ground—most of the time—and, until today, completed each of her assignments so smoothly that Tragar had considered promoting her to Final Cycle early.

That idea was now shot to Hades. And bedamned if Cherlon wouldn't get top honors as Most Exalted Educator this year, something he'd been trying to steal from Tragar for eons. That slimy weasel. Tragar wouldn't put it past that mushroom snorter to have placed this man in Aurora's path, just to thwart Tragar's exemplary record.

Queen of the fairies! The human had her so discombobulated she was eating animal flesh. Animal flesh! And his number one pupil didn't realize it!

"What to do? What?" He couldn't call her home. Not now. Once she deliberately downed the human libation, Tragar knew his perfect record was spoiled. Until the alcohol's arousing affects wound their way through her system, there was no reaching her.

Tragar's fuzzy ears drooped. So very disappointed, he was. His arms dropped to the ground, kicking up a billowing ball of dust. Knuckles dragging, he paced, contemplating the probable ruin of his star student. The light had gone out of his day.

"Clouds. All clouds. Dreary, so awfully dreary."

⸺⬥⸺

LUNGS FULL TO BURSTING, Aurora held her breath, waiting for the gorgeous human in front of her to make up his mind. It wasn't supposed to be this difficult to seduce a man, was it? Wasn't supposed to take this long, surely.

Staring at the delectable morsel who towered over her a good foot, she was actually glad her assignment was a bust. So what if the penalty was banishment to the Underworld for an eon or two? A few nights in Charlie's arms might just be worth it.

Oh, who was she kidding? Of course it would be worth it. Just the thought of his name had her fingers curling into her palms and her shoulder blades twitching. She couldn't believe the way she'd just touched him, trailing her nails across his wrist, up the textured fabric of his jacket. Why, he probably thought she was a floozy. Or worse, a tramp-stamped tart.

Well, so what? She wanted him and...and...damn the damn goat! Aurora was going after her man.

Charlie just stood there, staring at her, moving her almost as much as the alcohol. Maybe more. Looking into his eyes, so deep, so dark, she was lost, utterly lost.

She tried to ignore the tension gathering throughout her body and figure out why he hadn't answered her. Maybe she hadn't asked him right. Trixie always said human men were stupid. Maybe Charlie didn't understand what she wanted.

Maybe she hadn't used the correct words.

She rose onto her toes and placed her hands on his shoulders. Pulling him down, she spoke in his ear. "Charlie, would you like to have sex with me?"

THREE

Fairy

FAIRY (ALSO FAERIE, Fairye, Fay, Fae or Fey, among others) – n., *Any number of mystical, magical beings who inhabit various realms; they are said to dance in the moonlight, impart either luck or calamity (according to their purpose), and can be quite mischievous.*

HIS HEAD TURNED SO FAST his nose bumped against Aurora's cheek. Charlie gripped her around the waist and lifted her off the floor until their eyes were level. "Are you certain?" He fairly growled, "Don't tempt me if you don't mean it."

Warmth from his hands seeped into her body. "I would like it ever so much."

The startled look left his face and his lips widened in an appealing grin as he set her on her feet and reached for her hand. "Lovely lady, your wish is my—"

"Professor! Professor Morigan!"

The strident tone screeched like a gargoyle, gonging through her head, dazing Aurora for a moment. She gripped Charlie's hand in order to remain upright. He immediately put his arm around her and pulled her close. His unique brand of heat cascaded through her, blocking everything else... buffering her from the abrasive assault these other humans were to wont to make. Somehow, her Charlie's presence acted like an auric shield, protecting her from interfering energies.

Perhaps she'd been hasty, citing her wish to final in Astrologic Studies. The longer she remained near him, the more Aurora was thinking the field of Inter-Personal Dynamics between Humans and Mystic Imps seemed a more suitable calling.

When the ringing in her ears subsided, Aurora realized her Charlie was talking with three ancient crones who had the same wrinkly face set amidst various colors of hair and a man of middle years with lots of clothes on. Bright white clothes with shiny gold ribbons and pins.

"Just telling Captain Williams how you promised to give us a private little star party tonight. He'd like to join us, if you don't mind."

"Oh. Well, um, maybe tomorrow..." Charlie's voice trailed off, and he looked between her and the expectant people around them.

Star party? She almost levitated with excitement.

The thought of having sex with Charlie in the stars made flunking her assignment doubly worthwhile. She hadn't been to a party in the stars for ages. The last time her lineage had gathered off Rigel, her older brother Rion pulled the wings off a spacefly. Mother had been so mortified she sent them all home early. Since being grown, Aurora's studies kept her too busy to party but she just loved visiting the stars. She pulled on his arm, downright gleeful. "Oh yes, let's do the star party."

He looked surprised. "Really? *Now?*"

"I absolutely adore the stars. We can still have sex—"

CHARLES COUGHED LOUDLY THEN SQUEEZED her against him. "Well, ladies, Captain, it looks like I'll be your guide to the stars tonight. One constellation tour coming up. If you'll lead the way, Captain, to the best viewing area on deck?"

"Constellation tour? What?" grumped the old woman with hair the color of blueberries. "That's not right. You're supposed to—"

"Thank you, Charles," the frailest one said, interrupting her sister's confusing complaint. She stood and leaned on her cane, her poor pate almost bald. "It's nice of you to take time out from your vacation." When the two next to her looked eager to complain further, she pressed, "Sisters? Isn't that right?"

"Well, I wasn't so sure you still wanted to, *Professor Morigan*. The way you skipped dessert and all, standing there, staring at..." Orange-haired Harriet looked pointedly at the woman tucked into his side.

"That little hussy."

Huh. The blue-haired one was a bitch, calling his woman names, Charles thought, holding Aurora even closer. He wanted to tell blue-hair she could shove her disparaging remarks right up her tight, wrinkly—

"Can it, Mabel." The almost-no-haired one gave him a wink and poked her sister in the side with her cane.

His stance relaxed. This one was all right in his book.

"Yes, Hazel." Chastised, blue-haired Mabel waved the damn napkin in front of her face again, brushing away her embarrassment at being called to task in front of others. Served her right, damn biddy.

Harriet continued, glossing over the interruption. "The way you were acting so distracted and all, I wasn't sure you'd still be up for this."

Oh, I'm up for it all right. Charles looked at the petite woman by his side. Her wide, excited smile was small compensation to his disappointed dick.

He couldn't believe she wanted him to give a damn constellation tour to a gaggle of shipboard geezers, not when the two of them could be sprawled on his bed, buck naked, moaning all over each other. God, how he wanted her lips around him. How he wanted to lick every part of her. He could imagine her taste, so light and delicate...shimmering, like her barely there dress. A shudder ripped through him. Good thing he'd skipped dessert after all. His stomach couldn't take much more.

Not only did she have him by the balls, but this small fey creature tied his gut in knots unlike anything he'd experienced.

The captain led the vocal triplets and several other passengers who had gathered toward a side exit. The woman curled her arm around his and threaded their fingers together as they followed the entourage out of the dining room and onto an open-air deck. Wind whipped the sides of his jacket in every direction and he struggled to button it with his free hand while holding on to her with the other. No way was he letting go of his dinner companion and soon-to-be bed partner.

Walking at a leisurely pace to allow the others to get ahead of them, Charles said, "I didn't catch your name at dinner."

"That's because I didn't throw it." She laughed, hugging his arm and looking at him through the veil of her lashes. "I'm Aurora."

Ah, as in the colorful lights of the aurora borealis. It fit. "Well, my darling Aurora, you have certainly surprised me tonight."

"Dare I hope 'tis been in a good way?"

He heard the earnest inquiry. His feet slowed then stilled. He swung around to face her. "In a very good way."

"My response to you," she said in a quiet murmur that nevertheless reached his ears clearly, "surprises me too. In a grand and marvelous way."

The admission was all it took. He was toast.

Charles leaned down and pressed his lips against hers. Damn if she didn't float up to meet him.

The first touch of her lips was magic. In an instant, the vague, annoying feelings that had plagued his stomach vanished, coalescing into raging-hot desire. Pure need erupted and he backed her against the ship's railing, devouring her mouth with his.

The humid, windy air surrounded them, bringing a light chill to the back of his neck. He gripped her against him, wanting to shield her from the evening's dew. Her lips were soft, ripe, and his erection grew hard and thick as he plundered the inner recesses of her mouth.

Where had this sex-starved scientist sprung from? He didn't recognize himself. Instead of displaying the serious mien and calm façade Dr. Morigan presented to the world, he was acting like an out-of-control adolescent. His cock felt like a red giant about to explode. And he loved it. Allowing his desire free rein for the first time in years, he—

She squirmed in his arms, the action subduing

his intensity. He dragged his lips from hers, breathing heavily, and placed one arm behind her on the ship's railing. "What...too fast? I'm sorry... I can't seem..." In his excitement, he was almost panting, unable to catch his breath. He squeezed the metal rail, trying to regain control. "I'll slow down. I promise. Didn't mean..."

She brought up one hand between them and traced his lips, still wet from her tongue, halting his blathering. "Oh no. I adore what you're doing. You could hasten your pace and not find fault with me. 'Tis only that...that..." She glanced behind her at the unending midnight depths surrounding them then quickly swung her gaze back to his.

"That?" he prompted.

Charles had the distinct feeling she'd been about to utter something completely different when she gripped his forearm with her free hand and finally offered, "It's just that I wanted to touch you but my hand was trapped between us."

Realizing—despite her slight ambiguity—that he hadn't scared her off, he relaxed his death grip on the rail. His tongue slipped out to meet her still-questing fingers. Instead of tasting a hint of salt air as he expected, her skin was sweet. Sweet and smooth. His lips wrapped around one of her fingers and he pulled it into his mouth, running his tongue over the slender digit and sucking gently. Then with more fervor.

"You taste of," he murmured against succulent flesh, "of..."

He struggled to describe it. Sugar? Honey? No, neither was right. Letting her finger slide from his mouth, Charles placed a hand against her cheek and tilted her head to the side. He gazed at her moonlit eyes then bent to lick the silky skin of her jaw. Ambrosia. Magnolias. He ran his tongue down the side of her neck, addicted but past caring. Euphoria. Rainbows.

Huh? Rainbows? Was he out of his ever-lovin' mind? How could anyone taste of rainbows? Or euphoria?

Unwilling to follow that line of thought, he pushed everything away in his single-minded determination to taste all of her. Trailing his tongue past her collarbone, he moved toward her breast.

The filmy dress provided no barrier at all. His tongue easily found her nipple through the silken sheen and he savored her. He didn't care if he was insane. This experience, this woman...it all felt wonderful, intense. Better than anything he could remember.

Aha! He finally recognized her flavor. "Nectar," he spoke around her nipple, trying to fill his mouth and express the chaotic thoughts churning through him all at once. "Aurora, you taste of the nectar of the gods."

Showing her appreciation of his comment—or possibly of his talented tongue—she thrust her breast against his mouth and sank her nails into his scalp. God, the minute pain from those tiny arcs pressing into his skin combined with what his mouth was doing tilted his world off its axis. He reached for the hem of her dress, grazed his fingers up the smooth, sparkly skin of her leg—

Sparkly? Huh?

But yes, his fingers were tingling like sparklers lit on the 4th of July. Brilliant. His hand rose higher, mouth sucked harder and—

"Professor Morrrrrgaaaaaan! Where are yooouuuu?"

Holy hell.

Where was his restraint? His composure? He forced his trembling lips to release her breast and covered the moist mound with his free hand.

Damn. He was expected to conduct himself in a professional and coherent manner in a few moments.

He stopped caressing her leg with a hand that damn near shook, let her dress fall into place and brought his mouth back to hers. He was breathing as if he'd run a marathon. The sharp point of her nipple pressed into his palm and his fingers instinctively contracted, holding the slight weight of her breast. The hollow feeling was back in his gut.

"Dammit," he mumbled against her lips. "I don't want to stop."

"Then don't." She licked his lips then plunged her tongue straight into his mouth.

The groan he made could've been heard in the Andromeda Galaxy, a good 2.5 million light years away.

AURORA SMILED at the sound and continued to kiss him. Had her lips and tongue ever received such a fierce, excited plundering? Such possession?

She'd already known she liked Charlie's heat and his sunny hair and big, brawny body. Now she knew she *more* than liked his taste and the way he touched her—with care at first, as though she were something precious and fragile and might shatter. Then with barely restrained force, as though Charlie knew if she broke he'd be the one to find and shelter the pieces.

"Ohhh-hoooo, Proooofessssorrrr! Are you *cominnnggg*?"

He pulled back with a grimace. "I guess *that* will have to wait for later."

Laughing, Aurora grabbed his hand and took off toward the others, practically flying over the deck. "Come on, dear Charlie! Our star party awaits!"

When they arrived at the bow of the ship, a small crowd milled about, waiting for the impromptu star party. Were they as excited as she was? The choppy waves sounded louder here as the giant vessel sliced its way through the water. Charlie kept a firm grasp on her hand and walked toward the captain who was easy to spot, his white uniform reflecting the soft moonlight.

"Ah, there you are, Professor Morigan." The captain greeted them with a casual salute. "I took the liberty of asking the waitstaff to bring some refreshments. Now that dinner is over, I'm officially off-duty for the night. What better way to relax than with a sky full of stars and a rye and ginger, eh?"

Charlie shot her a wry look, accompanied by a wink, before responding to the captain. She bit back a giggle.

"Right you are, sir. We've got such a flat horizon here at sea and a cloudless sky tonight. It should make for excellent viewing. I only hope I can do your beautiful night sky justice."

"Drink up, everyone! Drink up!" a familiar, antique voice enthused. "Wine an' bubbly's on us tonight."

"Mabel! Quit drizzling away our cruise funds— and to strangers!"

"Stow it, Harry." *Thump* went the cane.

Two waiters carrying loaded trays meandered through the small crowd, dispensing glasses of wine and champagne as well as taking orders for other drinks. Aurora snagged a fluted glass when the waiter passed by. Sipping the alcohol, she gave herself up to the pleasure of the night. Time enough tomorrow to decide what she was going to do about Tragar and the blasted goat assignment, *after* Charlie's star party. For now, the decision had been taken out of her hands the moment she saw him again at dinner.

"Let's get started then, eh?" the captain said. "Everyone, if you'll gather around, we're fortunate to have a professional astronomer in our midst who's going to grace us with a tour of the stars tonight."

She heard Charlie cough self-consciously as he relinquished her hand and dug into his pocket for what turned out to be a small laser pointer. Aurora leaned against his back, reaching her arms around his middle to give him a quick hug for confidence. He was so unlike the cocksure, know-it-all male fairies back home. His nervousness made her want him even more.

"All right, folks." He cleared his throat then pointed a neon green laser beam into the heavens. "We'll start with a couple of the brighter objects that are out tonight. If everyone will look just above the moon, you'll see a slightly reddish object. That's Mars."

SEVERAL *OOOOOO'S* and *ahhhhh's* followed his statement. "The god of war, right?" someone asked.

"Ha! War? I always say make love." *Thump!* "Not war."

"Hazel! We're in public."

"Don't be such a prude, Mabes. I've made plenty of love in my day, I tell you." *Thump! Thump!* "Plenty."

Charles felt Aurora shaking with silent laughter and he struggled not to join her. These three broads were worse than the college kids who frequented his constellation tours back home.

"Ahem. Let's see…if you'll all turn around, there's Saturn, in the constellation of Cancer the Crab, above the horizon a bit."

Aurora snuggled closer, creating rings around his thoughts. She had her thumbs tucked into his waistband and her hands rested against his hip bones. Just a few inches more and she'd be able to feel the hard ridge of his erection.

"Saturn? It looks like a bright star to me." The comment came from the far side of the deck.

"You can see the planet, and even its ring structure, in a good set of binoculars or a small telescope. For now, I'll just point out basic star formations, all right?" The green laser beam shot into the sky again. Aurora nestled along his back, her diminutive form belying the amount of heat their proximity generated. He tried—valiantly—to sound coherent to their fellow observers. "Do you see the backward question mark just beneath Cancer on the horizon? That's the head of Leo the Lion. We'll be able to see the rest of it in awhile, as the earth rotates. On the other side of Cancer the Crab is Gemini. The Twins."

As he articulated each one, the laser followed its outline, indicating the exact location. Concentrating on what he was saying proved nigh impossible, given how his mind kept replaying images of the beauty behind him—naked and in complete abandon. Given how his tongue kept tripping over itself, recalling the taste of her skin, the bead of flesh topping her breast...

Luckily for him, he knew the night sky better than most folks did their own neighborhood. "And right above that is Taurus the Bull, and then we have—"

"What about Capricorn, Professor? Can you point it out?"

"I'd love to, but it's not visible this time of year. Each of—"

"But Capricorn is our sign and our birthday is next week. Why can't we see it?"

By now he recognized the irritable tone of her voice and took an educated guess on the speaker. "Well, Miss Harriet, the zodiac constellations are called your *Sun* signs," Charles began, letting his arm take a break from holding the laser pointer. He took a moment to reach around and run his hand down Aurora's side, lightly squeezing the outside of her thigh. She *mmmmm*ed and wiggled against him. Minx.

"I know that. I've been going to astrologers for years, you know," Harriet chastised.

"The term Sun sign," he explained patiently, "means that our Sun was in that specific constellation on the day of your birth, which is why you can't see it right now. It would be visible during the daytime, but the Sun's natural light blocks it out."

"But I wanted to—"

"Quit pestering Professor Charles, Harry. He's doing his job. A true Capricorn trait, so you've told me more than once."

"All I see is how stubborn you're being. Another trait, I'll have you know. No wonder your knees are bad, Hazel. You're inflexible. Just like the old goat you—"

"Ah." Hoping to stave off the forthcoming argument, Charles interrupted. "If everyone will look to the side of Gemini and Taurus, we have a widely recognized constellation. Anyone know what that is?"

"Orion!" Several voices responded.

"That's right. Orion the Hunter. These four stars make up his body." Charles reluctantly relinquished his grasp on Aurora and pointed to the stars. Her softly mewed protest went straight to his groin. "This bright star located at his knee is Rigel. It's the seventh brightest star in our nighttime sky. And there's the Orion Nebula, which is below his belt in the sword. It's—"

"Is it true that it wasn't his sword at first? But his penis?"

"Hazel! How could you?" Mabel complained.

"I'm so embarrassed!" wailed Harriet.

"Grow up, girls. Penis, vagina, breasts, buttocks…

everybody here knows who's got what and where it goes."

"Oh lordy..."

"Professor Charles? His sword?" Hazel asked again.

Aurora's hands left the side of his hips, and under the cover of his suit jacket she slipped her fingers into his front pockets. Sweat beaded his upper lip. He wanted to remove his jacket but didn't dare. Dark or not, the bulge in his pants was sure to draw attention, and all this talk of penises certainly wasn't helping. "Well, ah, yes. When the constellations were first identified, it was before man had fashioned steel swords. I have heard that Orion's sword was originally considered..." *His heavy, throbbing dick.* "His, uh, phallus. Moving on—"

"Are there any other planets out tonight?" Saved by the man in the white suit. The captain had procured a pair of binoculars and was staring intently at the sky.

"None that we can see. Uranus just set, right before we came out, but it can't be seen by the naked..." After allowing them to linger in his pockets only a moment, Aurora pulled her hands free. What next? Her fingers crawled across his hips and met in the center, tracing down the outline of his buttocks. Then she brought them up the seam of his pants— in between his ass cheeks!—setting off all kinds of nuclear reactions in his own sword. The laser pointer jerked in his hand, abruptly shifting to another part of the sky.

"*Eye!*" he choked out on an unmanly scream. "Naked eye." Naked? Gulp. Butt clenching, Charles marshaled his breathing, his concentration being spun out past the Pinwheel Galaxy. "Umm, just south of Orion's, ahem, *sword*, is Lepus the Rabbit."

Quick as a bunny, her hands left the crevice of his ass and snaked around into his front pockets again. Then they zoomed south. The thin material lining the inside of his pockets did nothing to dull the touch of her fingers gliding against his length, pressing around him, measuring, investigating. Thank God he'd left his jacket on. When her just slightly hesitant touch ventured over the swollen head of his penis, Charles couldn't hold back a groan.

Unexpectedly, her teasing hands ceased their torture. The pent-up air burst from his lungs. Good God, he'd had enough. Wrenching her fingers out of his pockets, he grabbed her hand and pulled her in front of him. Guiding her into his chest, he leaned down and whispered, "Turnabout is fair play. Now stand here and behave."

"Aye. Your command is my most heartfelt wish." The delightful sprite nestled against him, pushing her bottom into his groin. He bit back a growl.

"That's wicked!" A teenager had edged his way closer. He spoke with crisp, fast diction, identifying himself as British rather than American. "I've seen the rabbit shape on the moon before but I didn't know there was a rabbit constellation. Sick, man!"

"Yeah, uh…" Charles tamped down the sexual vibrations raging in his body and strove to make sense. "Uh, some cultures say Orion is hunting the hare, others say he's aiming his bow at Taurus."

Fortunately that comment started a spate of conversation about ancient cultures and mythology, allowing Charles a moment to gain his bearings. He unbuttoned his jacket and turned Aurora to face him, inhaling her heady, floral fragrance and wondering if he would ever be the same. Certainly he'd never look at the sky in the same way again.

Under the cover of darkness, he slid his hand along the length of her spine and cupped one cheek of her ass. Smooth. Firm. A handful. He was in pure heaven. Of their own accord, his fingers twitched inward, coming to rest at the crease of her buttocks. He tried to remember the next constellation he meant to point out, but one thought knocked everything else from his mind.

"You're not wearing any underwear," he whispered as his fingers slid farther inside the furrow between her legs, drawing the fabric of her dress with them.

She arched her back, pushing her core toward his questing fingers. Her hands went around his waist. "I never do."

"Oh God." His voice sounded much louder than he'd expected. Several heads turned their way. "Ah,

God…God, uh, surely did design a wondrous blanket of stars for us to gaze upon each night. Didn't he?"

Murmurs of agreement followed his statement and no one seemed to suspect anything out of the ordinary, thank the starry heavens. Charles inched his sinful fingers forward, sensing her heat and wanting nothing more than to dive inside.

FOUR

Magic

MAGIC – may be n., adj. or v., depending upon usage, *Supernatural forces applied with intent and purpose to cause a specified outcome. May also be done as parlor tricks for entertainment purposes, but true mystics value their abilities beyond that of pedestrian amusements.*

IT DIDN'T TAKE Aurora long to figure out her idea of a star party differed significantly from the humans'. Which in some ways was a relief. At a crowded fey party, everyone would have been exclaiming over Charlie's size and vying for his attention, and she didn't want to share him. Even with other humans nearby, the cover of night gave her the courage to touch and explore him.

And explore him she did. Especially since she'd

grown bold a few minutes ago and traced him with her fingers, cupped him in her hand.

"Well, I for one don't see a rabbit. A bunny. Or a durn-tootin' hare! I thought you were going to *read* the stars for us."

"Yes, Professor Morigan. Harriet's right. I didn't count on getting a crick in my neck looking up all durn night. I was expecting to *hear* my horoscope. *Humpf.*"

Thump. Thump. "Have another bottle of wine, Mabes. Then maybe you'll quit your whining."

"Maybe I will!"

Luxuriating in his heat, in the divine probe of his fingers questing over her bottom, Aurora never wanted to leave. Her position or this place. She smoothed her cheek against Charlie's chest and the loud thundering of his heart soothed her like a lullaby. Aroused her too. He squeezed one side of her butt then released her and cleared his throat.

"Ladies, are you familiar with the Seven Sisters?"

Aurora held her breath.

"It's also known as the Pleiades. This open star cluster is almost straight overhead."

His arm moved across her shoulders to point with the laser. With his other arm anchored across her lower back, he pulled her tight to him. The hard ridge of his erection pressed insistently against her stomach. Her core felt so hollow, so empty. Oh, how she wished she were taller. She wiggled closer and whimpered in her throat. In response, his hand splayed across her shoulder blades and mashed her breasts against his chest. Comets and kismet, how wonderful it felt.

"Oooo, you mean the Little Dipper?" one of the ancient women asked.

"A lot of people mistakenly think that, Miss Mabel, but no, that's the Seven Sisters."

She loved hearing Charlie talk about the gateway to her homeland.

"But I've always been told it's the Little Dipper too!" The braying shrill was adamant and it boomed past Aurora's sensitive ear drums. She pressed one ear flat against Charlie's heart, appreciating the steady, muffled beat all over again. "Ever since I was a little girl and all."

"Yeah, and we all know how long *that's* been. Ha!" *Thump!*

"The Seven Sisters?" another observer commented. "You know, I've heard some people on Earth claim to be from there. Is there any truth to that?"

She shifted to his side and gazed at the stars in question. They seemed to be winking at her.

"Of course not," he told his audience. "That's just a ridiculous old wives' tale."

"I still say it's the Little Dipper. *Harumph!*"

Slugs and spaceblisters, but that woman's voice was piercing!

"Little Dipper, schmipper. The man is a professional, Harry. Give it a rest."

"But it is a dip-*hipper*," one of them hiccuped, "and it's *little*. I just don't see how it can't be—"

"You two are as stubborn as all get-out. Another one of those Capricorn traits you're so fond of, I wager. Ha!" *Thump!*

"Yes, well so is being socially responsible, Hazel. And your snide comments are certainly not!"

"Land sakes, Harry, you know I think that astrology claptrap is pure hogwash. I only know so much from listening to you two yak about it every year."

"Gripe about it all you want, Harriet and I think it's remark—" *hiccup* "—ably accurate." Demonstrating her newfound knowledge, the woman pointed to the heavens with the pale napkin she'd swiped from the dinner table. "After Professor Morigan showed us Saturn, I remembered the sign of Capricorn is ruled by Saturn."

"Huh?" Poor Charlie seemed perplexed at his loss of control. Aurora hugged him tighter.

"And it's an *Earth* sign, so you can just put that in your girdle, Hazel, and smoke it."

"I've had enough, both of you. If Mother were here she'd be appalled by your behavior." The old woman banged her cane on the deck, punctuating her irritation. "Captain, Professor Charles, thank you for an enjoyable evening. I'm hitting the hay before I do something totally out of character and wring their necks. Or better yet, throw 'em both overboard. Ha!"

Spunky Hazel inclined her head toward her sisters, who had gathered a small crowd around them and were discussing astrology—and the merits of Merlot. "This may well be the last cruise I take with them. Next year, think I'll celebrate my birthday alone. Thank you again, Professor. It's certainly been educational. Maybe the captain can arrange a nice little massage for me at the spa tomorrow, to work the crick out of *my* neck? From my pain-in-the-ass sisters, you know. Ha! They were booked when I tried to arrange something earlier, but I bet I can count on you to pull rank, right?"

Aurora watched the captain tip his head in acknowledgment then down the rest of his drink. "I think this will be it for me as well, eh? Morning comes early on the high seas. Thank you, Professor... Mrs. Morigan? Allow me, Miss Hazel, to escort you to your cabin. And tomorrow, I'll be happy to arrange..."

His words faded as, with a slight weave to his walk, the captain and his elderly companion led a small exodus away from the observation deck. Only a few stragglers remained, waiting to hear anything else Charlie might share.

"Well, folks, I guess it's about time we conclude our lesson. If you'll notice, our good ol' lion Leo has—"

"Look!" the teenager called out. "A falling star! Wicked!"

"Actually, that's not a *fmmptt*—"

Aurora raised her hand to Charlie's lips and halted his technical explanation of falling space rock. "Allow them to believe," she whispered. "Humans need that."

He appeared startled by her words. After a moment of searching her eyes, he kissed her fingertips and she drew them away. "Yes, on any given night, you might see one or two dozen *falling stars*."

After sharing this bit of information, he looked at her, as if checking for her approval. She nodded with pleasure. Her initial suspicions were right—her Charlie was a good man.

Aurora was glad she'd kept quiet about the other cause for apparent falling stars—fairies entering Earth's atmosphere. She didn't want to scare him off before she got to know him better. A lot better.

The teenager and his parents walked over. "You give a wonderful program, sir," the father spoke up. "Cheers to you and your wife for sharing it with us tonight."

⟨○⟩

PICKING at his pointy teeth with the still-green twig, Tragar rolled his large, bulbous eyes, staring at the scene being acted out on the big boat. It hurt to watch. "Star student no more. No more."

The gravelly sounding words escaped past a throat thick with disappointment.

What did Aurora see in that human? The man

was big and hairy—never mind the fact Tragar had hair coiling out of *his* ears and nose—and the human was stupid. Couldn't the man tell that Aurora didn't belong?

It was her job to complete her assignment then return home. She wasn't supposed to lose sight of her training and her upbringing and hang all over the large man like a nymphet. Had she no pride?

A gargantuan sneeze caught him off guard. His nose twitched, curled. Tragar could smell her arousal from here...400 light years away. "Disgusting. So disgusting."

What was he to do? As long as she was affected by the alcohol, there would be no reaching her. And what would he do if her attraction to the human didn't wane? "Insane. All insane."

He could lose his post over this. Should he contact her mother? His ears shuddered at the thought. That had to be a last resort. Perhaps he could speak with one of her siblings? Maybe they—

"No. Heavens, no!" They were as likely to turn him into a toadstool as help him.

He spit the chewed twig from his mouth and scratched the side of his nose. Aurora's scent was growing stronger. He sneezed again, swaying the trunks of several nearby trees. Why did he have to be so attuned to his students? He had to find something to get rid of the stench. Where was a good dung beetle when one needed it?

Perhaps he would simply wait until she no

longer wanted the human and *then* call her back. Alcohol or not, she couldn't stay this aroused forever. Another sneeze built...

Aaa-CHOOOO!

By the queen's wings! "Why me? Why?"

———————◦◦———————

"LET'S get out of here, *wife*." Charlie placed strong emphasis on the last word, echoing the erroneous label, and earning a laugh from Aurora. "After the last hour of torture, I need to have you all to myself."

"I believe I know a place where we can be alone." Maybe her fruitless search throughout the ship would prove useful.

"Your cabin?" Charlie asked, looking at her with a hopeful expression. "Mine?"

"Someplace better." Aurora had noticed over the course of the evening, with Charlie touching her, she wasn't nearly as intimidated by the vast ocean. Unlike the shallow ponds proliferating her homeworld, the seemingly infinite, black depths typically brought forth all manner of apprehension, but with Charlie close by, the unease abated. And there was one place she desperately wanted to share with him. A place she hadn't been able to fully appreciate, her silly nerves causing a fast retreat earlier.

"Better? I like the sound of that."

"As do I." She took his hand and unhurriedly

walked along the deck. "I had no expectations of meeting someone like you today."

"That makes two of us." He hugged her to his side. "Any second thoughts?"

"Second thoughts?" It took her a moment to discern his meaning. "About having sex? Oh no. I'm looking forward to it. Vastly so!"

"God, you're refreshing. No woman has ever talked so openly to me before. I like it."

"You're easy to talk to, Charlie."

"And that's another thing. I'm used to being Charles or Dr. Morigan. When you call me *Charlie*, I feel like a kid again."

"Is that a good thing?"

"Considering how I'm as randy as a teenager, how I *didn't* discourage those folks from believing in falling stars, and how I'm loving every minute of tonight, I'd call it a good thing. A very good thing indeed. Think I've been spending way too much time behind my desk at work."

Swinging their joined hands, she invited, "Tell me about your work. I know you're an *astrologer*." The last word was accompanied by a tug on his arm.

"God forbid. I think that must be the bane of every self-respecting astronomer—being confused for a charlatan astrologer."

"Oh, I don't know. Maybe they aren't *all* bad."

In the dim light, he looked crestfallen. "Don't tell me you believe in all that horoscope nonsense?"

Aurora paused in their shipboard stroll to pull

her hand from his. She ran her fingers over his chest. Toying with the long, silky fabric knotted around his neck, she said, "Not necessarily *all* of it perhaps, but I've learned to be open-minded about things."

He reached up and helped her untie the knot. "Such as?"

"Things I'm not familiar with." *Such as human men.* "Or...things I simply don't know anything about." *Such as sex with human men.*

"But horoscopes? Astrology? That stuff is just drivel. A pure waste of time and money."

"Maybe someday you'll meet a fairy, one who'll make it her life's ambition to teach you about things you know nothing of..." She played with the top button on his shirt and let the suggestion hang in the air.

"A fairy, huh?" Thankfully, he didn't laugh, and he abandoned his stubborn position on ancient star science. "I'd rather *you* taught me."

Loosening the button from its hole, she ran her fingers along the edge of his shirt, absorbing the heat beneath. "I think that can be arranged."

CHARLES SLID his gaze over the deck, confirming they had privacy. Fortunately, the open-air swimming pool where they'd stopped was devoid of people.

From the muted music in the distance, most of the still-awake passengers likely populated the casino or the nearby dance-karaoke bar given the familiar, if muted, beat of someone belting out "(I Can't Get No) Satisfaction".

The hard, rocking melody thrummed through him, energizing, exciting.

Ironic, how the lyrics conveyed the exact opposite sentiment darting through his mind: if only he'd known how very satisfying it would be, to run into a stranger aboard a ship and experience such an instant attraction, he might've vacationed—for real —years sooner.

Ah, Charles, his inner wiseass remarked in an accent similar to their captain's, *but not just any stranger, eh? Only* this *one.*

"Aurora, Aurora," he murmured. "What is it about you?"

"Aye?"

"You utterly captivate me. And that's a fanciful notion." Especially for one not given to fancy. Only to facts.

The brisk wind coming off the ocean breezed past them, stirring her long hair.

A few strands had escaped the messy knot and he wound them around his hand. They were mahogany, dark and rich. Simple strands of brown hair. Nothing more.

Then how was it they seemed to have a life of their own? Winding themselves around *his* fingers, caressing his wrists—and *glowing*? A trick of the light, surely. They couldn't be luminescent. But damn if they didn't look that way. Like gold from a flaming fire, her hair—as did the rest of her—appeared magical, enticing him back to childhood and long-forgotten dreams.

"Dreams," he pondered aloud, entranced with the motion of her hair on his wrist, the back of his hand. The breeze, nothing more. Right? "Aurora, I do believe you're bringing to the surface ones I'd all but abandoned." Consigned to the Dumpster of life.

"Me?" Her top teeth dug into her bottom lip before her smile broke free. "Really? I'm exceedingly pleased to hear that. Everyone should have dreams, ones they never forget or lose sight of. Tell me yours?"

He left off staring at her hair and focused on her face. Drinking her into his soul. Rather than feeling impatient at the delay, he wanted to stave off that final orgasmic culmination, wanted to prolong and savor every second she'd grant him. "Your eyes. They're amazing," he murmured then confessed, "When I was a boy, my favorite aunt gave me a board game. It was full of princes and castles, fire-breathing dragons and damsels in distress."

"Do I remind you of that because you think I'm distressed?" She seemed disheartened by the idea.

"The opposite. You make me remember the Wee Folk, the Toadstool Dwellers, the whimsical flying fairies I always wanted to quest with."

Her brow burrowed. "Quest with? I'm unsure of your intended meaning." She flashed him a smile to rival Sirius, the brightest star beyond the Sun. "But I love how it sounds. Tell me more?"

"The game had Quests and Triumphs. Each Prince chose a helper, a partner." Mystified at how clearly the decades-old memories flooded in, Charles disentangled his hand and stepped away, toward the railing where he firmly anchored both. Though his fingers clenched cold metal, it didn't stall the thrumming up his arms from the odd fire her hair possessed. *Am I losing my mind?* His gaze shot to the slight woman beside him, waiting expectantly. *Or finding my sanity?*

She leaned against his shoulder and sighed. "Your voice is like smoke on velvet. You give me shivers, Charlie."

He chuckled in awe. "All those stupid years and wasted dollars on cartons of cigarettes to the rescue."

His one teenage rebellion. Smoked like a steamship for fifteen years. Finally stopped when he realized his parents weren't going to ask him to, and one of his students gave him a lecture on the evils of smoking—then showed him a picture of her father, dead at fifty-three from lung cancer.

"You're sad again," she said softly.

How did she do that? "Again?"

"Uh-huh. I noticed earlier, at dinner." When he'd been thinking of his parents and lost opportunities?

"You're amazingly perceptive." One arm snaked around her waist. Lightning struck through him. "And I confess, you give me shivers too."

Her laughter was like confetti, little pieces of joy and light, raining down on him. "And now you're happy again."

"That I am." And he couldn't wait to have her. The pressure filling his groin hadn't waned during their exchange. If anything it had increased, the sensations of her exploring fingers remaining, her rainbow scent and the openness he felt with her only amping the attraction.

Yet though he longed to see her naked, caress her bare body—taste her cream—part of him was reluctant to move. To end this oddly compelling interlude.

What if he took her and the magic ended? What if they weren't sexually compatible? What if she decided a big, hulking, stuffy scientist wasn't her cup of torrid tea and said *thanks* and *bye* after their encounter? Leaving him an orgasm or two richer but bereft of her presence?

What if the magic vanished—just when he was just starting to believe again?

AURORA HADN'T a clue as to what Charlie might be thinking, she only sensed how his thoughts made him *feel*. If she hadn't been so attuned to him she might've missed it, but he was special—to her at least.

None of the other human males had Charlie's brand of heat. She'd noticed that when the solicitous man guided her to the table where the various waiters delivered her food and drink. And the captain? He'd been lukewarm at best, his mood relaxed and jovial. But Charlie? Now *he* fascinated her.

Her studies on Interplanetary Species Interactions had been more lacking than she could've suspected.

Trixie would tell her to just pounce on him—let their loins unite and extinguish the burn. Quit worrying about emotions when erotic ecstasy loomed.

But although Aurora yearned to stroke his body all over, kiss and sample his lips, his toes—and everything in between—she yearned to know his mind too. Especially what caused that lift in his spirits when he shared about his quest game—and what caused his mood to crater so swiftly.

"Charlie? What happened with your Triumphs and Quests? Did you win?" And casting caution to the immense, impenetrable ocean because drawing attention to her unusual qualities probably wasn't wise but she couldn't stop herself from wanting to know, she asked, "Why did my eyes remind you of the game?"

His tense grip on the rail loosened and Charlie drew her in front of him, both of them facing the ever-changing, ever-constant ocean. Bracketing her within his arms, he groaned. "This is going to sound horribly juvenile, but they're the same color the Enchantress possessed. She was my favorite card. I used to sleep with her under my pillow and pretend the quests were real. That I could be the brave and strong Prince and live in a magical Kingdom, if only I believed enough."

"She sounds lovely. Yet why does sadness mar your memories of her?"

"Because, my inquisitive sprite, fairy tales are for children and I outgrew mine long ago." Hands to her hips, he drew her flush against him, his erection insistent against her lower back. "Outgrew my childhood, that is. The cravings you create in me are totally grown up. Manly in the extreme."

Aurora turned in his arms, slid one hip seductively—she hoped—against his shaft. Her Charlie was being stubborn, unwilling to, or uncomfortable about, revealing why he no longer believed in dreams. Luckily for him, Aurora was willing to wait.

They had all night, longer if they both chose. After all, if she never completed her assignment, maybe she could stay here forever...

Look up, my child. The unexpected notion sounded much like her mother, a total impossibility as her honored matriarch never ventured beyond their homeworld. Nevertheless, Aurora's gaze traveled upward.

The blinking stars studding the inky sky shone brilliantly everywhere she looked, reminding her of the majesty and splendor of the heavens from which she'd descended mere hours ago.

An odd inkling nudged her.

Focusing on Regulus, the star shining from Leo's chest, directly below Saturn and seventy-seven light years away, Aurora tested her magic, pleased as a pixie when the pinprick of light stopped moving— when they all did. Just *halted*. Ceased spinning and marking the passage of time.

"Moonbeams and morning glories, how very marvelous. It works here too! I'm ever so glad."

"Hmmm?"

Her magic had caught up with her—and Aurora had just used it to give her and Charlie *all the time in the world*.

"OH, NOTHING OF CONSEQUENCE," Aurora murmured, placing her hands at his neck and firmly massaging his nape. "Dear Charlie, your muscles are as tense as a ticked troll's."

Surprised when her analogy wrung a chuckle from him, given the turn of his thoughts, Charles determined to put off worrying. To stop contemplating the future and *what ifs*, and instead concentrate on savoring tonight. Every damn second. And he intended to start by satisfying the lovely lady rubbing his neck with such abandon he could've easily fallen over the rail and expired a happy, happy man.

"Past few years, it seems like I've been so busy

between work and research, I've forgotten how to relax. Tonight, with you, has been wonderful."

At his words, her beautiful amethyst eyes shone with pleasure. Her fingers on his neck sent coils of desire zooming south.

"So, what manner of academia do you study, *Professor*?"

"Every time I've heard that tonight, I think I'm on *Gilligan's Island*," he laughed.

Her expressive face mirrored confusion. "You're not one for pop-culture references, are you? Never mind then. I work in extrasolar planetary research. Most recently, I've been analyzing stars' gravitational fluctuations—"

"Toadstools and telescopes, Charlie, you study the heavens!"

He laughed at that. "I do my best. Locating exoplanets is an exciting field. While a few discoveries can be credited to straight telescope viewing, multitudes are made based on other methods such as pulsar timing, radial velocity and orbital transits. There've been a number of significant discoveries coming off the large Keck telescopes in Hawaii. That's why I'm so interested in working there. Hence traveling for an interview as one of their resident astronomers. The equipment I have access to is good, but this would be infinitely better."

During his explanation, her hands roved lower and wrapped themselves in the ends of his tie. She tugged, bringing his face level with hers. "I regret to admit I have absolutely, positively no idea what you just said, but I'm impressed nevertheless. You sound so sexy, imparting those scientific thing-a-ma-gummies. Tell me more," she invited, kissing his lips.

"Nah. That's beyond enough about me." He reluctantly pulled back. "What about you? You're not traveling alone, are you?" Why hadn't he thought to ask sooner? "Did you meet up with anyone on board? Friends? Family?"

"Maybe you can be both!" Her quip ended with a groan. "Dear me, that was very forward. Forget I uttered that." And before he could claim no offense taken, she rushed on. "I'm here on my own, aye." Then after a slight hesitation, "In truth, I'm on assignment."

"Assignment? Oh, you're a reporter?"

"Umm, one could say that. I do hope to be reporting..." She paused then gave him a mischievous wink. "Reporting back to my sister tales of the fantastic sex we're going to have."

"Damn, but you're amazing. And don't I need to expand my vocabulary?" But at least he knew she had a sister. He tried again—after spilling his guts, it was only fair she shared some dirt. Or at least an entrail or two. "It's unusual to travel solo on a cruise ship."

"Is it now? Yet aren't you?" She started playing with his shirt once more, dipping her fingers in between the buttons and caressing his stomach, causing his muscles to contract.

"Yeah, but that's because I've got that interview. Good thing I had enough vacation time for this ridiculously long cruise." Five days there, another five back, and a week touring the islands. Should he tell her the rest? What the hell? He was pretty sure he was getting laid either way. "The crux of it is, I'm too chicken to fly."

"Really? I *love* flying. Adore it!" He heard a wistful note in her voice.

"I can't fathom it. Scares the shit out of me. Why else would I take a month off this summer, supposedly for vacation, when I really just didn't want to get on a plane? God, I can't believe I'm telling you this."

"Maybe you just haven't flown with the right person yet."

"Maybe." Charles noticed her looking toward the pool, and was eager to change the subject. "Are you contemplating a midnight swim?"

Now that had possibilities!

"Oh no." Her fingers left his shirt, dammit, and she strolled forward, weaving around the lounge chairs, touching each as she passed. Over her shoulder, she gave him come-hither looks with every other step. "In actuality, I'm not comfortable around a lot of water. The black abyss scares *me* silly."

"Then why come on a cruise?"

She shrugged, a dainty lift of one shoulder that dropped the neckline of her dress two inches. "That is a rather pertinent question, isn't it? Because I don't really enjoy swimming or," he watched her tongue reach out and caress her lips, "getting wet."

God, she aroused him. In four strides he caught up with her. "Woman, if you're even half as wet as I am hard, we're both in for one hell of a ride."

Instead of scaring her off, his words excited her. Eyes narrowed, nostrils flared. "I am—so very wet for you. Are you ready for me?"

"More than you'll ever know." He traced the swell of her breast through her dress, his mouth watering at the remembered taste. His dick danced in his pants, ready to waltz in and salsa with her slit.

"I think I do know. Follow me, Charlie?"

"To hell and back," he promised.

"Nay, to heaven. That's where angels and fairies and children tread." Trembling from his touch, she backed up a step, turned and flew into a darkened corridor and down a staircase.

Shoving lounge chairs out of his way, he stayed close on her heels. There were so many things he wanted to know. Why come on a cruise if she didn't like water? Why did she act so innocent and unschooled one moment then so damn seductive and knowing the next?

Where had she been all his life?

It took all his concentration to follow her progress through the ship. She moved swiftly, as if she knew every inch of the large vessel. Giving the noisy casino a wide berth, she skirted around it and into a sparsely populated nightclub, stopping a moment to grab two champagne glasses from a tray at the bar before ducking outside.

The bartender yelled after her, and without missing a beat Charles slammed his card key on the counter. "Women!" He shrugged, running a hand over the back of his neck, pretending not to notice how his shirt was half undone. "And they call *us* impatient?"

Mollified, the guy grinned and swiped. "Thanks, mate."

Pocketing the card, he zoomed after her, speeding down first one corridor then another, thrilled he hadn't lost her trail. Because somehow, some impossible way, splotches of the dark floor shimmered up at him, little glittery sparkles high-lighting the swift tread of her dainty feet.

Intentionally slowing his pace, and his heart rate, once he realized he wouldn't lose her, Charles followed the luminescent pathway, attempting *not* to decipher how she'd made her footprints appear.

"Charlie!" Her voice came from ahead. "Did you take a wrong turn?"

Ethereal, mystical footprints aside, nice to know she hadn't forgotten about him. He rounded a corner and found her waiting at the entrance to the closed spa.

"Here? The spa?" For some reason, he'd never equated heaven with facials.

"Trust me. And prepare yourself to dream again." Pushing the door open with her hip, she flowed through the waiting room, past the deserted gym and outside onto a lounging area at the stern of the ship. Inset yellow lanterns lit the perimeter of the deck.

If the captain was serious about stargazing, they really needed to replace those yellow bulbs with red. *Scientific analysis—off*, Charles ordered his brain. *Lusty libido, on, on, on!*

She set the champagne on a table between two lounge chairs and twirled around, holding her arms up to the sky. "Is it not glorious? It's my favorite part of the entire ship. I wanted to share it with you."

Retracing his steps, Charles looked inside the doorframe and found what he wanted. With a flick of the switch, he blackened the lights, leaving the area illuminated by the stars and nothing else. Wrenching off his jacket, he threw it on one of the chairs.

"Aurora? Are we still going to do this?" His voice sounded rough, abrupt. The smooth scientist was gone. In his place was a wild man, his cock so damn stiff he could jackhammer a hole through the deck. He probably would, if she changed her mind.

FIVE

Make-Believe

MAKE-BELIEVE – n. or adj., *A common pastime of the young—and young at heart; involves suspending belief in the here and now and allowing one's mind to create pleasurable, fantastical circumstances. Often used as an escape mechanism or for sheer enjoyment.*

"SO, POPS, WHAT'D SHE DRINK?" The pink-haired, bubblegum-chewing pixie sat on the back of a dragonfly, zooming around his ears.

Tragar thought hard. What did the humans call that sparkly libation? "Bubbles. Golden. With bubbles."

"Champagne?" *Chomp, chomp* went the gum. "Anything else? It's important."

"Grapes. Fermented, green-skinned grapes." His lips puckered at the thought.

"Tragar, you silly troll, that's nothing. Wine and

champagne? We can metabolize fruit-based beverages in our sleep. That kind of alcohol isn't affecting her at all." Trixie kicked the sides of her ride and whooshed by his ear, tugging on an errant hair as she passed.

She always had been the most difficult one of the bunch. He should've called Rion or, heavens save him, their *mother*. "Not affecting? Not?"

"Nah, it's gotta be the hard stuff. Grain-based and distilled. And even then, it only messes with our libidos at certain altitudes." *Smack!* She flew in front of his face and landed between his eyes.

"What then? What?" He rubbed his ear where it still hurt, wishing he'd called anyone but Trixie. Wondering how she knew so much about alcoholic beverages.

"I don't know...maybe she's batty about this human. But it's not the liquor." *Chomp, chomp.*

Cross-eyed, he watched her blow a bubble with the offensive human-manufactured gum. *Pop!*

"Zeus knows she's overdue for a fling." *Chomp.* "She probably just needs to get her rocks off then she'll be ready to come home. Guess there goes your Teacher-of-the-Year award."

Another obnoxious bubble emerged from between smirking lips, a fancy double one this time.

Pop-pop!

The bubblegum bubble landed in his ear and Trixie zoomed away, laughing.

AURORA STOPPED SPINNING and watched Charlie approach. His white shirt reflected eerily in the starlight, and the long ends of his silky tie dangled from his neck. Shadowed skin showed between the edges of his shirt where she'd unbuttoned it.

Just seeing that, her mouth went dry.

Like a predator, he advanced, stopping inches away. Their eyes locked and she swallowed.

His warmth enveloped her, banishing the night's chill. Despite the allure of his heat, Aurora's feet scooted backward, not stopping until the ship's rail pressed into her back. "I brought the champagne on the off chance I became all apoplexed and so nervous I froze. Now I find I don't care. I want you, Charlie. I may not do everything right, but I want to do it all with you."

Still standing in the middle of the deck, he fisted his hands. An astonished look came over his face. "You're not a virgin, are you?"

"No, but neither have I—"

He lunged forward and wrapped his arms around her, capturing her mouth and stopping the flow of words. His lips were hot on hers, his tongue full and wet as it stroked against hers. He tasted of every fantasy and secret longing she'd ever had. Of the forgotten, of the never known. Of *right*. He tasted and kissed exactly right. This...*this* is what she'd craved from the moment she landed against him.

Charlie's big hands worked the neckline of her dress, easing the material past one shoulder and down her arm. Releasing her mouth, he saw where the sheer fabric had caught on the swells of her breasts and gingerly tugged until it rested on her hips, freeing her arms and leaving her torso exposed.

Under his silent scrutiny, both her nipples beaded and her slight breasts grew heavy, full with longing. "Touch me again there, if you please. With your tongue."

"Gladly." Bracing one warm palm at her back, his head swooped down and he took her nipple between his lips, running his tongue over the hardened tip and gently biting with his teeth. Exquisite sensations exploded in her belly. This was better than coasting on clouds or riding on raindrops!

Edgy from desire, she pushed him away and shoved the sides of his shirt apart, wrenching the remaining buttons from their holes. The moment his chest was bared, she sighed, witnessing majesty in all its perfection.

Her mind and tongue tangled as coherent thought—and speech—proved a trial. "Oh Charlie, thou art so very beautiful." Her fingers traced a path through the light covering of hair, starting at his collarbones, down past his pectoral muscles and across his firm stomach. Heat gathered in her hands, streaked up her arms. "And hot...thou—*you* are so exquisitely hot."

Gripping her shoulders, he turned her and secured both her hands around the rail in front of them. With him at her back, the view wasn't intimidating, was—if she were completely honest with herself—invigorating. All that beautiful, unknown splendor...

"Hold on, sweetheart. If we don't do something about it soon, we're both liable to go up in flames."

He pressed his chest against her bare back, the skin-to-skin contact scorching. The wind tossed her long dress around her legs, the glossy cloth teasing her with its nebulous caress. Charlie's erection rubbed against her butt and moisture pooled between her legs. His hands cupped her breasts, thumbs rubbing over her nipples, his attentions so much stronger and surer than any she'd known before.

"Your touch is heaven," she told him, "pure heaven." As she stood there, unsteady on her feet, the ship's wake trailing out behind them, Aurora looked deep into the sky and thanked her lucky stars for this assignment.

SHOULD HE PINCH HIMSELF? Nah. Pinching the beauty before him was proof enough.

Charles stood, trembling, in the starlight with his shirt undone and his arms wrapped around the most delicate and desirable creature he'd ever met. He must be the luckiest bastard alive.

The gentle swells of her breasts filled his palms perfectly. He kneaded the soft flesh, growing impossibly hard at the sight of her nude torso reflecting the starlight. With one hand, he tilted her chin to the side and pressed his lips against her mouth. His tongue swiped over her lips and inside when they parted, sipping her nectar. He swallowed her down. Then again, his palms kneading in tune with his stroking tongue. His hips joined the symphony, rocking in time, and if he didn't do something else—and quick—his dick was going to play the part of the fat lady and the concert was going to be over.

Too damn soon!

He forced his hips and hands to still, took one last sip and slid from her inviting mouth. "God, you're gorgeous."

Relinquishing his hold on her breasts, Charles hiked her right leg in his hand and placed her foot on the lower railing—

Her *bare* foot.

A quick glance down confirmed she hadn't just stepped out of sandals...or anything. "Aurora, did you lose your shoes overboard?"

"Um, noooo. Fair— Uh, my family—we never wear them. We aren't on our feet all that much."

No shoes. All damn day—and night. *No shoes.* Damn again. Around this lovely sprite, his powers of perception were puny. He'd never focused his attention below her flirty hemline.

Determined to rectify that now, Charles fell to his knees and anchored that lovely foot in place, opening her up.

Her long, filmy dress whipped over her spread thighs, a beacon in the bluish starlight. This close, her scent went straight to his head.

"Why do you stare so?" she asked on a soft sigh. "When I await your strong touch with my every weakened breath?"

What a poetic invitation she issued.

"In time," he vowed.

Time. Something Charles never savored anymore. Rush, rush, rush. To work, to class, damn grocery store so he didn't starve—or run out of cat litter again—more work, grade papers, write a new lecture series, analyze data on a new section of sky. Fall into bed exhausted—usually late—wake late and the rush started again.

That was no way to live, not when it kept him from truly *living*. Charles took a huge breath and paused, put everything on hold—his desire, his thoughts, his actions.

Only when he felt truly centered and one with the present moment did he proceed. Moving in super slo-mo, the kind that would do any sports broadcast replay proud, Charles consciously inhaled the night, paying particular attention to Aurora's unique aroma—her personal musk floated heavy on the air, tempting his tongue. But he held off. Instead lifting his hand to encircle her raised ankle. Delicate bones and sinew met his solid grasp.

She fluttered before him—no, that had to be her dress. Skimming his hand up over the radiant skin of her lower leg, he stopped at her knee and leaned in for a taste.

Though her cream drew him as nothing else, Charles instructed his erection to chill its jets and applied his tongue to the side of her leg.

"Mmmm!"

That was Aurora, but *mmmm* was right. So, he hadn't imagined that taste of ambrosia earlier, that aphrodisiac her skin wrought and delivered to his taste buds.

Hadn't imagined how her flavor went straight to his head—both of them—and made him feel weak and invincible all at once, the—

"Why must you prolong the torture?"

"Torture, sweet?" His tongue roved higher, to the back of her bent thigh. His opposite hand found its way to her upright leg and coiled round the front, keeping her in place.

She quivered in his grasp, against his tongue. "I've waited eons for a man to make my body sing, yet you persist in dallying!"

The complaint was so old-fashioned, so damn quaint that he laughed. Then could laugh no more as his nose won the battle over anticipation and delivered his face between her legs.

His tongue and lips took over from there, diving to the silky hollow at the apex.

NO LONGER DID she clasp the rail for support, to keep her steady in the face of the oceanic abyss. No, she clutched the rail to keep from *soaring*.

Though hidden from his view—in another dimension—her wings kept her balanced, giving Aurora the ability to release one hand from the ship, snap her fingers and catch the full glass of champagne as the stem zoomed into her waiting, curved hand.

All this she accomplished in a microsecond, gazing down at the big, clothed man centered on his knees between her thighs. His mouth hovered a moment, his gaze heating juices that ran thick and free. With a groan, he lurched forward and licked her.

Aurora could neither stop the squeal nor the liquid that splashed over the lip of the glass. Several droplets sprinkled her nude torso, sparkled up at her, the champagne shining golden against her pale skin.

"Oh Charrrr-leeee," she sighed as his tongue delved deep and mini-explosions lit up her pelvis.

The hands on each of her legs squeezed tight then released. He angled his head back and replaced his tongue with several fingertips, his other hand filling itself with one lobe of her bottom. Gazing up at her as his tongue swiped over glistening lips...his fingers searching, plumbing the depths of sensitive folds to the sounds of slick desire and her throaty gasps, he queried, "Oh whuuu-uuut?"

Laughing at his lighthearted response, choking on the arousal burning up from his swiped caress along her slit, Aurora held out the champagne glass, tilted her head back, and drizzled bubbly liquid over her breasts.

With a mental snap, she commanded the molecules to slow...and they obeyed, the beads of liquid meandering over the hard points of her nipples, down the swells of her breasts, past her stomach and bunched dress.

Watching the tiny trails, Charlie licked his lips again.

Aurora leaned into the strong hand at her butt, angled her neck and torso toward the sky and poured the rest of the contents out over her singing body, trusting Charlie to know the remaining notes.

He did.

Fingertips parted swollen folds. A broad palm squeezed a taut buttock and he shot off the deck and captured one beckoning, champagne-beaded nipple in his hot mouth with a throaty growl of lust to rival any Italian opera singer.

His tongue flicked hot and fast over her nipple, lips suctioned her sensitive flesh deep into his mouth. She sent the empty glass back to its full mate and wove her fingers through his spiky, sunny hair.

Clasped him to her breast.

To her heart.

And prayed they'd be granted more than just tonight.

CHARLES SUCKED nipple nectar as his fingers slid through dewy desire. All the while, his cock both applauded *and* pouted.

The single remaining cell in his brain that still functioned flashed out a *Red Alert*. If he and his naughty nymph were to finish their journey together, it was time to get the ol' boy strapped in for the ride.

Not sure how he'd made it this far, Charles rose shakily to his feet, aligned his left leg beneath hers, supporting her weight as she balanced on one foot. Hell, he'd had her in this position awhile.

He secured his hold on her ass and blindly reached past her dress, to coast his fingers over the slickness of her inner thighs. Her hips jerked forward and moisture covered his questing hand.

Against her shoulder, he whispered, "You're so very wet, so ready for me."

"That I am," she gasped.

The wind whipped her dress around them, waving it like a flag of surrender. Drenched, his fingers slid along her body, caressing her skin from the hollow above her clit, through the moist depths of her sex, to the tender area just beneath her anus.

With leisurely intent, he traced the path again. And again. Keeping a steady pace, he rubbed her entrance, preparing her. Faster now, his hips jerked in tandem with his fingers despite his mental orders to the contrary. *Halt!* his sluggish brain ordered again. But noooooo, his dick had other desires. He gritted his teeth, searching for control.

She writhed in his arms, angling against his swiftly pulsing hand. "Charlie, please."

"Please what?" he asked, slowing the frantic pace of his fingers and praying he wouldn't come in his pants.

"Touch me, wouldst thou!"

Sexual frustration made him abrupt. "Good god, woman, what do you think I'm doing?"

"But 'tis not the exact touch I crave." Her speech had gone all Shakespearean on him again. It was so damn weird. And so damn arousing. As though he plundered a medieval maiden. Fulfilled fantasies and dreams he'd had for so long, fantasies that were so deeply ingrained, responding in kind was the most natural thing in the world. "Aye, my fair maid, enlighten me. What manner of touch shall I grant thee?"

"My arse. I want..." She pushed her butt against his groin, sending bursts of white lightning straight to his cock. Twisting her head, practically bent over in half, her long hair flew out and wrapped around him, ensnaring him. With breath gone ragged, she cried out, "I want thy fingers upon my arse!"

Given how he'd just been kneading the area under discussion, he suspected she was asking for a different touch altogether. Who could deny an invitation such as that? Certainly not any scientist worth his salt. Or a prince reaching for dreams.

Charles rimmed the edges of her honeyed entrance one last time before pressing his middle finger against the nerve bundle at the top and sliding his thumb and palm along her cleft, not stopping until the pad of his thumb rested at the rosette of her anus.

Covered in her juices, he circled the puckered hole before entering. His finger spasmed against her clit. She moaned and ground herself against his touch. Licking her neck, he asked, "Like this?"

"Ummm." Rocking her hips from side to side, she circled over his fingers. He felt her muscles clenching and unclenching around him, drawing him deeper. "Aye, only..."

She broke off, heaved a sigh, opened the muscles of her rectum and pushed against him until he was embedded to the hilt.

He felt his control slipping. "Only...what?" he growled, pressing his mouth to her neck.

"Only there's more to be had and I want..." She swiveled her hips against his hand again.

"Say it, Aurora. Tell me." The wind blew her hair against his face, tangling several strands between his lips. He tongued them away. There were two places his cock could go and pray God she picked one of them fast. "Do you want me here?" He pistoned his middle finger. "Or here?" He fluttered his thumb.

"Aye! Yes, I mean, I'd like your cock inside my queynte."

The arm around her torso jerked reflexively. Lucky for her he'd read Chaucer. Several times over as a pubescent teenager.

But Aurora was already providing breathy elucidation. "Umm...my...my lady bits."

"Don't have to tell me twice, sweetheart." With a groan, he pulled his hand from the secret depths of her body and unfastened his pants. Pushing them down, he fisted his engorged erection, flinching at how sensitive the shaft.

Tightening his hold, he ran the tip down the crack bisecting her taut buttocks, to her drenched center. Already his pole shone, slick with her cream. He aligned himself, held the base steady, took a deep breath—

"Aw, dammit! Dammit, dammit! Condom."

Condom! How could he've forgotten? *Because I've been thinkin' for ya*, his cock seemed to wink up at him. Glistening, flushed and poised between the pale globes of her inviting ass, his shaft swelled in his hand, protesting the unexpected interruption, while Charles stood there, straining in place.

"Straiten your eyes."

Huh?

"Close your eyes, Charlie! Quick!"

Automatically, he obeyed. Hearing himself

panting like a dog in the blackness, he strove for control, gripped his rod in a vise and tried not to howl. Did ships have all-night pharmacies? Could he claim dire medical emergency and have a box of condoms airlifted to—

"All done! Continue on!"

Huh?

"Open your eyes!"

Dully, he did and color him blind if a damn condom hadn't appeared on his dick.

A lime green, glow-in-the-dark one at that!

That did it. He had to be dreaming, hallucinating, locked in the loony bin. All those late nights looking through telescopes and staring at stars, all those hours analyzing spectral data collected by computers had finally caught up with him.

But if he was locked away in a padded cell, how was it he could taste the salt air on his tongue, feel the overwhelming rush of freedom and see the starlit beauty bent before him, beckoning him onward?

Her lilting yet breathy, "Your pillicock's covered in the contemporary fashion, is it not? So why do you persist in delay—"

Not one to look a gift horse—or green condom— in the mouth, Charles guided his stiff—and shimmering!—erection to her entrance, halting her speech. Had he ever before been this big? This hard? This *green*?

With an amazed chuckle, and to the chorus of

her whimpered sigh, he released the hold on his dick and eased inside the snug passage whose walls yielded with such excruciating reluctance it *felt* to Charles as if he were her first.

Once embedded to his groin, he stilled, striving not to lose it—and waiting for her response.

Hoping and wishing on stars he wasn't imagining tonight.

"AHHH, YESSS," Aurora breathed as her body stretched to accommodate Charlie. The reality of his invasion more wonderful than she'd suspected possible. She gasped at the overwhelming sense of fullness he delivered, lurching against him in exhausted relief.

The torture was finally over. Big, strong, sexy Charlie filled every empty part of her. After tonight it would be her turn to fill him. To brighten those dark spots shadowing his happiness, but for now...

The rippling muscles of her tunnel started milking his shaft, drawing him deeper, ever deeper.

"Sweet heaven." His voice was hoarse. "Sweet, sweet..."

No longer willing to settle for soft or serene, not with the new sensations storming her loins, Aurora let loose a primal yell—which was totally unlike her —and arched forward then back, pounding into him over and over. Feeling both savage and sultry— another first—Aurora held on to the rail to keep from floating off into the night and flailed her hips, taking in his body with wild abandon.

"Aurora. My God!" His hot mouth opened over her shoulder. The flat of his tongue bathed her skin, sending fiery chills to her toes. His fingers groped past her hip and down her abdomen. Scraped through her curls to delve alongside puffy inner lips, his fingertips stroking her outside flesh with every pump and thrust he delivered.

She started to vibrate, coils of tingly energy thrumming outward from where they were joined, coalescing at that spot where—

"Charlie!" She squirmed against him, itchy, aching. It was too fast! Would be over too soon. Intense beyond her ken, her realm. "Char—"

Teeth at her earlobe startled the word to a stop. He licked a trail around the shell, slowed his ferocious thrusts. "Calm down, 'Rora. It's all right."

Still embedded in her, he wound one arm across her waist then lurched back until they fell on a lounge chair. Holding her tightly atop him, her nipples pointing skyward, legs straddling his, Charlie brushed his hands across her breasts and stomach, over her mons, the top of her thighs.

Consciously, she savored every smoking-hot inch of her studly scientist.

"You still with me?" he asked.

Too fired up to answer any other way, she clenched her feminine muscles around him, propped her feet atop his legs—noticing his pants were still on—and ground her fingernails in the muscles of his upper thighs.

"Hold on, baby." Before the words were out, he resumed plunging in and out of her at the speed of light. One hand kneaded a breast, the other slipped between her legs. As she stared at the twinkling, blinking canopy above them, Charlie spread the feminine folds surrounding his driving erection and pressed several fingertips to the top of her slit. That was it. He didn't move his hand—but he didn't have to, the rocking, sliding motion of his shaft shifting...things...just...enough...

The twin motions of his thrusting and fingers caused her to coil into a ball of writhing need. A whimper escaped her lips and she joined in, bucking wildly in his arms.

"Oh yeah...that's it. We're both gonna fly now." His deep voice held her prisoner.

"Charlieeee," she cried out when the muscles beneath her shoulder blades twitched and nearly took wing. The zinging throb centered under his hand took root and spread outward, encompassing every limb and inch of skin till she feared she would melt.

When combustion seemed imminent, *ka-pow!* She detonated beneath his touch and around his body, her release flooding past his shaft and slicking his hand.

No floating back to earth or rest for her, nuh-uh.

Charlie's gyrating pelvis halted as he grunted his

appreciation for the involuntary convulsions constricting around his erection, gingerly slid his fingers off her clit—to *her* hissed appreciation—and wrapped both arms around her middle, locking their bodies together.

His hot exhalations gusted past her forehead. "Damn, Aurora. I swear you're glowing like your namesake."

She felt herself beam even brighter.

He strained beneath her, his shaft arrowing north inside her sex like a compass pointing the way home. But that was it. Other than his slight trembling, Charlie didn't make another move.

Naïve she might be in the ways of humans and orgasms, but she knew Charlie hadn't taken one for himself. "But you—" she began.

"Got to pause. Not yet...don't want to—" Defying his words, his hips lunged upward, lifting off the lounger and rocking his cock deep.

On a burst of semen and swearing, Charlie came in that condom she'd provided for their frolicking pleasure—thank the gods Trixie'd taught her that trick!

Just as fast, he groaned. "Dammit, didn't want to finish, not yet."

Though he hadn't softened, not that she could tell, Aurora felt the sinuous glide of his shaft as it eased past the walls of her tunnel, leaving her.

With a heartfelt groan rumbling from his chest, he turned her in his arms. She flowed over to her stomach then sat up, legs on either side, to straddle his muscular thighs.

"Ah, Aurora bore-*amazingly-magical*-alis! What you do to me."

What she did was quickly dispose of his spent condom and grant him a fresh one—lavender this time, not quite as bright—and prop her feet on the deck so she could have him inside again.

"You're still wearing too many clothes," she laughed, realizing neither of them were totally nude.

"A purple one now?" he muttered, holding the base of his penis erect with one hand, the other at her hip, guiding her in place.

Ahhh, the languid sensation that rolled over her when she sank down and took him inside to the root, tangling their pubic hair together and just... sitting there.

Toes curled, queynte clasping, heart and wings beating out such a fast tattoo, Aurora expected to perish from pleasure.

"Purple, by damn." His eyes smoldered up at her, one arm crossed behind his head, the other delving beneath her flared dress and finding her clit and resting atop the nerve bundle that had yet to relax. "Now I know I'm dreaming because this can't be real."

Flexing her legs, she began to ride him. No gallop through the heavens on any unicorn had ever felt this freeing. "Why is that?"

He surged into her, stomach muscles flexing, the

edges of his shirt and jacket falling to the side, exposing more of his tantalizing torso. "Because fantasies don't come true. Make-believe isn't—"

He broke off when her breathing hitched, her motions changed. She swallowed hard when she crested against his thumb, around his cock and over his groin.

"*Real.*" The whisper tore from his throat as he closed his eyes, whipped his hand from between her legs and delivered slick fingers to his mouth for a taste of her release. "By damn, this cannot be real."

But two minutes later it was Aurora surging wildly, dragging her nails down the center of his ridged chest and stomach, exclaiming, "Sex and solar flares, Charlie...again? So soon?" Wondering if it was possible. Trixie was right. Human sex was infinitely light years ahead of fairy sex.

Or maybe it was just... "Charlie!"

Kismet

KISMET – n., *Often equated with Destiny or Fate; a foregone outcome or set of circumstances that manifests despite all obstacles, or perhaps simply because a happy ending is written in the stars.*

CORONAL MASS EJECTION INDEED.

Charles reclined on the lounge chair, practically numb in the aftermath of his mind-blowing orgasms. He held Aurora snugly against his bare chest—having finally disposed of his shirt—her legs intertwined with his. She'd draped his jacket over them both. He'd straightened her dress and fastened his pants, but he still felt completely exposed.

He wanted to talk, to say something debonair, something impressive. Hell, he wanted to tell her that was the best damn sex session he'd ever engaged in.

And he wanted more. Much more. Of the orgasms, yes, but of her too.

She was kissing and nuzzling his chest while her fingers idly traced patterns across his muscles. Those late nights watching *Star Trek* reruns and doing push-ups every commercial had paid unexpected dividends—she seemed enthralled with his chest and shoulders.

He rubbed the dark spot on the back of her neck, one of several he'd inadvertently left—*him*, Dr. Control! His lips still tingled from being pressed against her defied-description shimmery skin during his climax.

"I didn't hurt you, did I?"

She stopped toying with his chest hair and looked up. "Hurt me? Not at all." Her slow smile was sultry sin wrapped in whimsy. How did she do that? "What makes you ask such a thing?"

"Because you're so small, so delicate. Ethereal." The complete opposite of him and his logic-oriented acquaintances and life. "I'm not used to women like you."

"What kind of women are you used to?" She bit her lip and glanced away. "There I go being forward again. I shouldn't have inquired about that. I do apologize."

"I don't mind." He thought of the few women he'd dated seriously—before his near miss with marriage. Intellectual, scientist types often with man-short hair who sometimes tended to be short on femininity too. Colorless women who didn't inspire or incite a fraction of the desire Aurora did. "Because you're the only woman I'm interested in." The only one he could fathom ever being interested in again.

Her eyes lit with pleasure. "You said you're from Arizona?"

"That's right." The sudden shift in topic surprised him. "It's just me and ol' Prick."

When he replayed what he'd said—to the accompaniment of her giggle—Charles coughed to cover the gaffe. "Prickly Pear, that is—my cat. I rescued the tom from a batch of cactus down the street when he was just a starved runt. Now we're buds." Only close friend he had these days, only one he *slept* with for certain. "If I could've smuggled him on board, I would have done it in a heartbeat. As it is, I bribed him with a case of caviar. And the neighbor's checking on him daily."

"You're a good man, Charlie Morigan. A kind man."

Unaccustomed to such staunch, confident praise —especially from one such as her...surreal, surprising and surprisingly astute he was about to find out.

To put the conversation back on neutral footing, Charles questioned, "What made you think of Arizona? Have you been there?"

"I found it on the map in the ship's library

earlier. I wanted to see where you live. That's in the middle of the desert, isn't it?"

He probably should return them both to his cabin for the afterglow, the after-sex, get-to-know-you banter he wasn't adept at, but with Aurora seemed all too easy. He knew he needed to relocate them off the lounger—and to a bed—but couldn't bring himself to move. Lying there was perfect, talking with her and gazing out at a night sky that'd never shone so brilliantly nor lasted so long. Too perfect to move. "While the Chihuahuan Desert covers part of the state, my home's further north, in the mountains."

"Really? I've always wanted to see a real mountain range. Flat pictures, even animated ones, and dimensional holograms simply don't do nature justice, wouldn't you agree? There's nothing like immersing oneself in the scents, sounds and textures to be had of—"

"Holograms?"

Though he could sense her blush, she waved off his incredulous query. "I live in the woods, surrounded by lush trees and colorful flowers." She gestured beyond the railing. "It's pleasing on the ocean, and I like how I've become more comfortable with it the longer we've been out here together, but I wouldn't want to live with so much water all the time. The occasional rainfall is delightful, but I'm a wood fair—uh, woodsy girl."

"I think you'd like my home." Strangely, he

wanted to take her there, show her his space, introduce her to Prick. "And trust me, we have plenty of trees."

If he took the astronomer position at Mauna Kea, he'd be on an island, *surrounded* by the water she wasn't overly fond of and...and... *Face it, buddy you probably won't see her again.* Suddenly the new job didn't appeal quite as much as before. "Where are you from? I neglected to ask earlier."

She seemed startled by his question. "Um. Oh, you know..."

No, he didn't. That's why he'd asked. "Aurora? Why so hesitant? You didn't break out of jail or run away from home?"

"Nothing so sinister, I promise you."

"Well then?"

"Mmm, I like to say I make my home in the stars. You know—Pleiades, Rigel, the Orion Nebula, Witch Head—"

He cut her off with a kiss. "A smartass, huh? I'm impressed you remembered so much. The way your hands were all over me, I don't know how you heard a thing I said."

"When the instructor speaks," she intoned then ruined it with a giggle, "I listen. In fact, I'm accounted a very good student, Professor."

"I'll say." Her recent words echoed in his head. "Wait a minute. I didn't discuss the Witch—"

She rose over his chest, bringing her lips to his.

"Is there anything else you'd like to teach me?" she asked with a seductive purr.

"Woman, you go from naïve to siren faster than a blink. But it won't distract me, not this time. How do you know about the Witch Head Nebula? It's not a common object."

She shrugged and looked away. "Did you not point it out during your constellation tour? I'm certain...I heard...thought..."

"No, I didn't. And why are you being so secretive?"

"Why are you being so stubborn? It truly doesn't matter."

"For some reason, I think it does. But I'll let it go." *For now.*

"Good." She settled against his chest again, trailing his damn tie across his pecs. Why hadn't he tossed it overboard yet? "You seem fascinated with that thing."

"Why do you wear so many clothes? Even on vacation you're all covered."

"I don't know. Guess I'm used to dressing this way for work. It didn't occur to me to change."

"Being industrious and a responsible employee is a commendable endeavor, to be sure, but..." She slipped the tie behind his nape and draped it over one shoulder, circling the end around his left nipple.

Charles stayed her restless hand, trapping it under his. "But?"

"I think you spend too much time working. When do you have fun?"

He released her and reached down to cup her ass. "I had fun tonight. Am having fun right now."

"As am I." Gazing into his eyes, a luminous smile lit her face. "When the ancient woman asked you about Orion's sword, I thought you..." She laughed.

"What?"

"I thought you were going to expire on the spot."

"Yeah, it felt that way. Between arguing about the Little Dipper, dodging their astrology questions about Capricorn and enduring your questing fingers—"

"Enduring?" she almost shrieked.

"Forgive me. Poor choice of words."

"I'll say."

"Should've used 'suffering'."

"Charlie! You...rodent!"

A rat? That was the worst thing she could call him? "Aurora! You...delight!" He kneaded the delightful handful in his palm.

She arched into his touch. "Quit trying to distract me."

"Yes ma'am." But like naughty schoolboys the world over, Charles kept right on distracting, filling his opposite hand with her other cheek.

"Now about those astrology questions." She squirmed into his hold. "I've been doing some thinking, Professor Morigan."

"Uh-oh. Sounds like I'm in deep rat shit now."

"Rat shit?" She giggled. "Trixie'll like that one. She's forever on the prowl for new Earth phrases."

Earth phrases? Could this conversation get any stranger? Bypassing that one in favor of learning more about her family and copping another feel, Charlie inquired, "Trixie? Who's she?"

"The sister I told you about. Back to that rat shit," she squirmed after uttering the coarse word, "uh, you're in...serious trouble."

Serious trouble? Now he was downright afraid to ask. His groping hands stilled their mission. "Yessss?"

"Stubborn. Ambitious. Sober and solemn about life. And work." She punctuated each statement with a light kiss to his chest. "You're starting to sound suspiciously like a Capricorn yourself."

IN THE STARLIGHT, Aurora's keen eyes saw the sheepish look appear on his face and an idea began to form. Outrageous, something she'd expect Trixie to do, but still...it just might work.

"You caught me. My birthday's tomorrow." He raised his arm and pressed a button on his time-piece, causing the face to illuminate. "Uh, today," he corrected with a smile then did a double take, flashing the readout again. "This can't be right. Is the battery dead? Come to think on it, I can't believe it's not dawn yet—"

Her fingers to his lips stopped the burgeoning

tirade. Knowing by now exactly what she needed to, that a lifetime with Charlie wouldn't be enough, Aurora looked out at Regulus. The faithful star—um, actually the planet they were on and not the star—hadn't rotated an inch. She flicked her fingers and set things—as in *time*—in motion again. "There now. Don't worry about your battery. Back to what you just said about your birthday. So you *are* a Capricorn?" She wanted to be 100 percent certain.

"Guilty as charged."

"I guess that means we're going to have to celebrate. Luckily for you, I have a few ideas."

And luckily for her, implementing her *other* idea could wait.

Running her hand all over his brawny body, she returned to the center to toy with his pants' zipper. "Tonight's the first time I've ever experienced such bliss."

"*Ever?* Had an orgasm, you mean? Tell me you don't mean you never—"

"No, I've done that. Just not thrice in one night." *Or with a human male.* "May we do it again? Now?"

He wiggled his hips. "Be my guest."

Aurora unfastened the waistband clasp and drew the zipper down. "May I?"

Without waiting for an answer, she crawled over him to make quick work of shedding his layers. "We need to do something about all these clothes you wear, Charlie-mine, as they are totally unnecessary."

"Totally," he gasped as she sought out her prize.

Upon reaching lengthening, rapidly firming flesh, she sighed. "You're so different. I never knew... Trixie was right. Oh stars and satellites, you make me so hot, I think I may burst into flames."

His satisfied laughter stopped the moment her lips wrapped around him.

THUMP. Thump.

Though half asleep, the familiar noise niggled his mind. Charles longed to roll over and tuck Aurora closer, but something prevented him from moving. He yawned. Stretched in place. Tried to settle back in.

Thump.

A well-oiled door swung open nearby.

The slight sound sufficed. He awoke with a start. Disoriented, he blinked and saw the amber-rose of dawn reflected on the water. "Aurora," he whispered. "Wake up."

She sighed and kissed his neck. "I'm awake. Dark matter and daisies, but you're warm."

"Aurora, sweetheart, we probably need to—"

"Fornicators!" The screech sounded directly above his head.

Thump. "Good heavens, Mabes. Put a sock in it."

"B-but Ha-Hazel, they've...they're—"

"Enjoyed themselves thoroughly if I'm any judge.

Now make like a wave and disperse before I tell the professor to feed you to the sharks."

Charles thought tossing the blue-haired witch overboard sounded like a plan. But he wasn't too sure the idea would fly with Aurora. Or the captain.

"I-I'm going to faint," the annoying woman threatened. "I've got to find Harriet. Oh my!" The door banged shut behind her with a thud.

"Sorry about that, dearies. Guess that's what years of repressed sexuality will do to a body." Hazel's wispy-bald pate appeared upside down above his head, her big grin surrounded by a wealth of wrinkles. *Character* lines. This broad had character. "Glad to see desire repression isn't something either of you have to worry about."

Relieved that his pants were on, if barely, Charles tried to rise but was jerked back down by pressure on his wrist. "What the—?"

Aurora sat up in front of him, a surprisingly serene expression on her face for one just caught *déshabille*. Placing her hand over his wrist, she looked at the sky. "I did it. Do you see, Tragar? I tied up the goat—and a very sexy one at that. And since—"

"Goat?" Charles croaked.

"Capricorn, the goat. Never mind. I promise to explain it all later," she whispered to him. In a louder voice, she continued. "I completed my assignment per your instructions. Since I may now choose the next one, I choose to stay here. With Charlie."

Charles glanced from his wrist to Aurora to Hazel and back to his wrist where his necktie was knotted around his arm and secured to the lounge chair. "Huh?"

"Way to go, girl." Hazel beamed at Aurora, thumping her cane up and down with glee. "You caught you a good one, if I'm any judge. From the first moment I saw you two together I thought your destiny was written in the stars. Ha!"

Aurora seemed to think the joke positively grand while Charles just lay there like a bump on a log—more specifically, like a lump on a lounger—confused as all get out.

"You just worked a little faster than I expected, Professor Charles," Hazel added with a wink. "After the most refreshing sleep of my life, I can see it's best if the sun rises without me today. I'll do what I can to ensure you have privacy for a few minutes more, but you might want to move things into your cabin before long." The cane thumped again and with a chuckle, she returned to the spa.

———❭◦❬———

"FAILED. SO SORRY. FAILED." Tragar hung his head, desolate to be standing before Queen Arlene and her king.

"No, Tragar, on the contrary, your star pupil did just as we desired."

Tugging on the hairy lobe of his right ear, Tragar

just stared as a ray of hope shot through him for the first time since he'd sent Aurora off on her last assignment. "Oh? Oh!"

The queen continued, her soft words flowing over him. "The good professor will be far too busy to continue his research. In truth, he'll soon be a devoted husband and eventually a doting father who will choose to take the recently offered full-time teaching position so he can be with his wonderful wife Aurora and daughter Splendor, instead of languishing hours away at the research lab as he has done much of his life.

"Had Charles Morigan, Ph.D. continued his current field of study… Well, suffice it to say that our homeworld is now secure from discovery for another millennium or so."

The king inclined his head in a nod of appreciation. "We're exceptionally pleased at how this evolved. So pleased in fact, that you, Tragar, will once again be receiving the esteemed Most Exalted Educator Award this cycle. Congratulations."

Cherlon's howl could be heard across the galaxy.

Tragar just smiled at the sound of his nemesis's frustration, scratched his nose and thanked the heavens for Miss Aurora, his star student extraordinaire.

Then he returned home to pry Trixie's blasted bubblegum out of his ear.

CHARLES LOOKED AT AURORA. "You tied me to the chair?" He gave his wrist a tug. "With my necktie?"

"I sincerely hope you don't mind. It was, ah, something I needed to do." She flushed a becoming shade of pink. Which unaccountably reminded him of green and purple condoms and their phenomenal night together.

"I don't mind at all, but I am a little disappointed."

"Disappointed? Whatever for?"

He hauled her forward for a quick kiss. "If there's any tying up to do, I think I'd rather be awake so I can enjoy it."

A mischievous sparkle lit her eyes. "Do you have additional neckties in your cabin?"

"That I do."

"Wonderful. Because I'd like to tell you some things—well, a great number of things—and I think I want you securely bound first."

"Seeing as how it's *my* birthday, I think it's my turn to bind you. To my bed. That's only fair, seeing as how you've had this old goat tied in knots since the moment he saw you."

Pleasure—and relief, if he wasn't mistaken—shaded her smile. "In truth?"

"Yes, *in truth,* my enchantress. Now help me get

this undone. We have a date—in my cabin—and I for one am eager to get going."

She bit her lip then nodded as if coming to an important decision. With a flick of her hand, the necktie fell away from his wrist. Without either of them touching it.

Stunned, Charles gazed into her amethyst eyes, their depths glinting with an intriguing combination of whimsy and mystery, shadowed by a touch of uncertainty. Uncertainty that cleared when he only blinked and said, "You're going to have to tell me how you did that."

"I will. After I tie you up. I promise."

"Give me a hint."

"It's magic," she whispered against his lips.

Magic. From the moment he'd seen her...magic.

THANKS FOR READING *STARLIGHT SEDUCTION*. I hope Charlie and Aurora's journey toward lasting love satisfied your inner romantic. If you have a chance to write a review, it's always appreciated. Reviews and word-of-mouth are the best things you can do for authors you enjoy.

MEANWHILE, laugh every day and savor the stars whenever you get a chance.

No Guts, No Gasms

I want him bad. Even though I shouldn't.

But I've obsessed all summer, watched those

tattooed muscles flex and sweat as he tends the grounds where I work, lusting from afar.

Soon he'll be gone.

Or I will; my internship ends next week.

So I better make my move—or live with regret. And I'd much rather live with the memory of his hands *all* over me.

6000 words • Sex with Strangers • Upbeat ending • Super Steamy

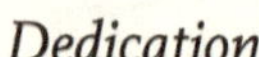

Dedication

Once again, to Mr. Lyons—thank you sweetheart, for all of the years, months, and minutes of assistance and support. One of these days (I hope!), I'll learn how to write and keep house at the same time. >^..^<

I was drove to it by a passion too impetuous
for me to resist.

                         –John Cleland, *Fanny Hill: Memoirs of a
Woman of Pleasure*

ONE

The Sexy Bad Boy
____

Because sometimes the sexy bad boy who seems so out of
reach...isn't.

HE'D JUST UPENDED SEX—I mean *six*—huge bags
that read *Mulch 'n' Manure*. Concealed behind two
layers of mirrored glass, I gazed outside the office
building's second-story window and watched the
sexy stud shovel shit.

I'd spent the last seven minutes hiding behind
binoculars, studying every close-up inch of tanned
skin visible in the eyepieces, analyzing both his tight
ass and his shoveling technique. Pathetic, I know.
But the tattoo-adorned naked torso below was so
worth a little patheticism.

God. I can't even justify my actions without

butchering the English language. Lame and boring, that was me, hiding up here. Alone...

It doesn't have to be that way, my increasingly loud inner vixen clamored. After ignoring the prodding from my naughtier side for almost twenty-two years, all I could do now was listen...and gaze at the sweaty, sculpted body below.

The shock of sand-white blond hair was a testament to his time outdoors. The bronzed muscles I drooled over, the pale blue eyes I dreamed over fueled my fantasies as nothing I'd ever known before.

My hands shook as I focused in on the detailed depiction of the sun tattoo adorning the broad curve of one deltoid. Jagged, daggerlike rays of orange and yellow streaked across the muscles of his upper arm, flexing every time he moved.

A bold tribal symbol was splayed over his opposite shoulder, but I couldn't get a bead on the design covering one pec. What was it? And what would it feel like to run my fingertips through the fine dusting of hair on his body, tracing the tattoos?

Heat swarmed through me, flushing my face and settling deep in my abdomen.

Wasn't I too young for hot flashes?

My breath flowed a little faster as I tilted my head, scanning the length of his strong back and hard butt (the latter covered in faded denim, darn it).

He'd arrived late. As the afternoon had worn on and my coworkers all left, I'd thought perhaps Travis

—of *Travis Taylor's Landscaping & Design*, according to the sign on his battered truck—might not show today, but I'd waited, hanging around long after quitting time.

My patience (or desperation) had paid off.

Last Friday, I'd finally worked up the courage to speak and we'd exchanged a few words, but I wanted a lot more than words.

I wanted his tongue.

In my mouth.

Licking across my skin.

Diving between my legs.

My body shook with the force of that wanting.

He was like a wild palomino stallion—untamed—and I wanted to ride him. But I'd always been afraid of horses.

No guts, no glory, my inner vixen taunted. I crammed the binoculars in the drawer and pulled out my purse. After powdering my nose (yeah, as if he'd ever get close enough to notice!) and freshening my lips with Sultry Summer Pink, I made a beeline for the source of every erotic fantasy I've had this summer.

TRAVIS WIPED a forearm across his dripping brow. It came away smeared with dirt. Damn. He'd been in such a rush, he'd left his bandanna in the truck. With the back of one glove, he mopped his forehead then glanced at the large glass doors...still no movement from inside the building.

Shit, he'd hurried for nothing. The straitlaced female he glimpsed most Friday afternoons must've already left. And wasn't he the fool for wasting time thinking about her?

She wasn't his usual bump an' grind.

But then, since quitting the hard stuff two years ago, his usual type left him limp.

It wasn't that he couldn't get it up, no problems there. Just that the *thought* of fucking the hard-edged women he'd partied with for years made him feel dirty even before the act was done. Much less started.

Which also made for a lot of long, lonely nights. Twenty-five months' worth to be exact. Ever since making the tough-as-jerky decision to clean up his act.

And what prompted *that* was the eye-opening reality of being seated three feet away from the first girl he'd ever kissed—a chaste, half-second cheek smack that had warmed his lips for a week. A pony-tailed sweetheart he hadn't seen in nearly two decades.

Only this time, they weren't eight and outside catching fireflies. No, she was frowning down her pert nose at him—over one very pregnant belly— and asking, "What happened, Travis, to the boy I knew? More than that, how can we clean you up? Get things moving in a different direction?"

This time she was seated across from him at a sterile desk—the pictures of her smiling family notwithstanding—because she'd been assigned as his new probation officer. One who specialized in substance abuse.

But *this* time, this very moment, it wasn't fireflies he was catching in the dark to innocently impress a girl, it was fireflies storming his gut, flaring bright and burning hot, a testament to his anything-but-innocent cravings for the *woman* he hoped to see today. The one he'd noticed all summer.

The buttoned-up beauty who smiled shyly and stopped just short of flirting...

Her tentative smile was pure heaven. And, hell, she about made his weekend every Friday. At least, jacking off to thoughts of her made his weekend.

Damn. He might have sworn off the pills and powder, put the illegal shit behind him, but if she had even a hint of the things he wanted to do to her body, she'd have his sorry ass arrested.

So why waste time contemplating a subdued female when his mind should be on work? He dropped the shovel and picked up the rake.

Now he had to spread manure with a fucking hard-on. *Smart, Trav, real smart.*

I PUSHED through the revolving doors and entered the sweltering August heat. Several steps down the concrete walkway and he was close enough to hear me. My heart was jackhammering in my chest, threatening to pound right past my ribs. *Be cool. Keep it casual.* Before I lost my nerve, I spoke up. "Looks like you're working late today."

The guy I'd been ogling all summer straightened and whipped around to face me. Droplets of perspiration flew from his hair. "So are you, I see."

His gloved fingers flexed on the handle of the rake. Up close, I could see the blocky, rugged cross spanning the left side of his chest, a decrepit skull lolling next to the base. A faded snake coiled from there to the right side of his stomach. I should have been disgusted; I hated snakes.

So why did I find it sexy?

Maybe it had something to do with the mass of muscles beneath the sinuous tattoo? Maybe I was just losing my mind...

"Nice tat," I said, trying not to obviously stare at the glistening, tanned skin and delineated biceps not four steps away. Heat from the concrete beneath my feet rose upward. The flesh beneath my skirt boiled.

He grinned, a flash of white teeth surrounded by a framework of sexy razor stubble. "Which one?"

I stared at the four distinct tattoos visible with his shirt off. As always, I found myself drawn to the newest-looking one on his left shoulder. "The sun."

"That's my favorite too."

"What's that one mean?" I pointed to the asymmetrical symbol.

"No clue. I was wasted when I got it."

At least he was honest. My eyes wandered over the inked drawings and my mouth watered. How I wanted to rip the rake from his grasp, throw it to the side and scrape my nails down his chest. I blinked, trying to erase the vision...the yearning.

"How long've you worked here?" He nodded toward the office complex.

You wanna get naked?

"Oh, um..." Good Lord. A few bulging muscles, a couple of hot tattoos, and I turn into a blathering idiot. "Just this summer. Internship. I graduate this month."

Now why had I told him that?

"Cool. Congratulations." He shifted. Muscles flexed. The sun's rays danced—both on his body and inside mine.

My loins fairly sizzled, the heartbeat in my crotch pulsing between my legs. I couldn't keep my eyes off his chiseled shoulder. "Where'd you get it?" I blurted.

"What? The tattoo?"

I nodded. Sweat erupted above my lips; I mashed them together, smearing the freshly applied lipstick.

"Electric Ed's Body Art and Piercings. Over on Montague. Are you thinking of getting one?"

You wanna get naked?

"Um. I might. A little graduation present. Maybe." Could I sound any dorkier?

He laughed and hefted the rake. "Something to shock the parents, is that it?"

I stood taller and forced myself to meet his gaze, sweat and pulsing pussy be damned. "No. Something for *me*."

"Whoa-ho! So the sex kitten has claws." His grin widened. "Maybe I'll see you over there sometime. Like tonight."

Was that a dare? *Sex kitten?!* "Maybe you will."

I gripped my purse to keep from tearing his jeans off.

My inner vixen wanted to get down-and-dirty in the dirt, but I restrained myself. Barely.

Before I hyperventilated and passed out—in a pile of freshly raked fertilizer—I sauntered (with a bit of extra hip action) toward my car.

Had I just made a not-quite date to meet Mr. Travis Landscaper at a tattoo parlor? *Tonight?*

<hr>

TWO HOURS LATER, fresh from a cold shower, Travis sat in the parking lot of Electric Ed's, drumming his fingers on the wheel and sucking on a Tic-Tac, wishing it was her clit.

What in the hell was he doing?

Lusting after a shy intern he had no business even thinking about? Waiting for her to mark her lovely skin? Hoping to ply her with liquor—in the guise of moral support—and plow into her?

How low could he sink?

As deep as she'd let him…

His cock twitched at the thought.

Hell, it had been a long day. Two of his guys had called in sick at the last minute—hungover, he'd bet. He should be at home, reclining in front of the tube, brewski in one hand, Whopper in the other. Handling his dick after that. Then bed.

Five a.m. came early.

Releasing his grip on the wheel, Travis reached for the ignition.

Then something, some*one*, caught his eye and he sat up, every muscle alert. He recognized her by the walk alone. Everything else was transformed.

Gone was the prim little knot; now her hair was swinging over her shoulders, loose and free. Shorter than he'd expected but wild, the strands waved around her head like a mane. Gone was the dark boxy suit, replaced by curve-hugging denim and a red halter top that left damn near all of her back exposed.

In a pair of worn cowboy boots, she glided straight up to the door and disappeared inside Ed's. Travis was out of the truck and after her in a flash.

TRAVIS SILENTLY CAME up behind her. For twenty minutes, he'd stealthily shadowed her around the tattoo shop's front room then the rest of the place while she scoured designs wallpapering every available space and flipped through several binders left on counters.

Part of him was curious—would she be looking for him or was she really planning to go under the iron? The crowd of patrons milling about had made it simple enough to follow her unseen, during which two things became apparent: he really thought she intended to mark her skin and she didn't appear to be casting covert glances over her shoulder seeking *him*.

When he couldn't decide whether her apparent self-confidence was a turn-on, or her lack of concern over whether or not he showed injured his pride, Travis knew it was time to make his move. That or leave without looking back. And since *that* was out of the question...he'd approached her.

"So what'd you decide on?" he asked near her ear, inhaling the light jasmine scent of her shampoo and feeling it settle in his lungs like a punch to the gut. "Have you picked something out?"

After jumping at the sound of his voice, she spun to face him and her eyes lit up like it was Christmas. "You came! I mean, *hi*."

Then she stood there, beaming, gazing at him as though Santa had just dropped him off in front of her fireplace. Trav felt about ten feet tall. "The tattoo?" he reminded, grinning.

"This one." She blushed and pointed to a wicked line drawing of a tiger. He approved. "I was born in the year of the Chinese tiger."

Travis winked. "Year of the cock."

Her eyes flared. "Are you getting another tattoo?"

"Not tonight. They're addictive. I've put myself on a tattoo moratorium until I turn thirty. Then I'll reconsider. See what skin is left...see what appeals."

"And that'll be when?" she fished.

Trav willingly took the bait. "A little less than two years."

"*Really?*"

"I know. I already look thirty. Hell, forty."

"No, you don't. Not anywhere near forty. Early thirties, maybe, but you're still gorgeous." She slapped a hand over her mouth.

So damn innocent. He leaned in close. *Are you a virgin?* "What'd you come here for?"

Good Girl Gone
Brave

And sometimes the girl who's always walked the line...
can't wait to cross it.

SHE WAS QUIET, evaluating him with her eyes, and Travis could tell she was weighing her response. "A tattoo," she finally said. "I'm here for a tattoo."

"Is that all?"

He watched as she licked her lips and assessed his body instead of answering. His skin sizzled—there was that look again. She was staring at him as if she'd been on a no-sugar diet for years and he was a seven-layer chocolate cake. Maybe after the tattoo he'd take her for dessert. *Eat her for dessert.* "Do you like chocolate?"

"Who doesn't?"

Her eyes said she knew they weren't talking

about food. Damn. He wanted to thrust his cock between her lips. He wanted to ride her mouth to completion, that alluring needs-kissing-and-fucking, lipstick-tinted mouth.

"Do you like it hard?" He had to test her. Could she keep up with him? Satisfy him?

Could he go slow enough to satisfy her?

"Hard?" She made a little sound in her throat, a cross between a moan and a hum. His dick stirred in response. "I, um, like my chocolate creamy but I..." She swallowed and dropped her gaze. It centered on his fly. "I like other things hard."

"Ready, little lady?" Some new guy, every inch of exposed skin on his arms and neck inked in intricate, colorful designs, interrupted. "The gal before you keeps waffling, so you're up next."

Three minutes later, she was straddling a chair, her upper back being prepped, her hands gripping his. "It's gonna hurt, isn't it? Crap. Maybe I should have taken some Tylenol?"

"Don't think it'd make a bit of difference, not now."

"Go ahead," she told the guy hovering at her shoulder. "I'm ready. I think."

Travis loved her hesitance. He loved her courage more. "You don't have to do this, you know. You could just get something pierced, save—"

"I want to. I need to." A buzzing sound emitted from beside the tattoo artist. She tensed when he touched the instrument to her right shoulder blade. But she didn't move away. "I'm tired of being boring."

"Who says you're boring?"

"My ex-boyfriend."

"He's a fucking idiot."

"What a sweet thing to say." She flinched and started breathing through her mouth...slow, measured exhalations. Deep inhalations. God, her mouth. A work of art. A dark, hollow cavern...made to encase his cock.

He watched her as long as he could, saying nothing, stripping her with his mind, fucking her with his gaze. Through the entire procedure, her eyes never left his. When the tattoo artist reached the tiger's tail and carved the long, curving line, she squeezed his fingers tighter.

"I want your soft pink lips wrapped around my dick," he said quietly, finally, partly to distract her. Mostly because he was a horny bastard. And wanted to make sure she knew it. "It's not your fault other men haven't seen the fire in you. Known how to feed the flames. Then put them out."

"I..." She bit her bottom lip, eyes blazing.

"All done." The guy behind her pushed to his feet. "Pay up and get a bed, you two. We're runnin' a business here, not a damn dating service."

MY SHOULDER BLADE stung like the devil, but when Travis placed his arm across my lower back and escorted me into the night, all I felt was the blood rushing between my inner thighs. I wanted him and I didn't care if he knew it. No guts, no glory...

Outside Electric Ed's, I turned to him. "Will you take me?"

"Home?"

Take me. I couldn't say it again. Instead, I stood on my tiptoes and kissed him, hoping he'd take over, hoping he'd know—

His mint-flavored tongue banished all thought.

He pressed his lips hard against mine and explored my mouth. After the way he'd undressed me with his eyes, aroused me with his words, I didn't need preliminaries.

This wouldn't be the floundering attempts of a frat boy or the first-time sprint of a high school senior. This would be sex with a sexy stranger. Something to remember, to learn from, to relive every Friday afternoon for the next two years, maybe longer. My inner muscles clenched, beyond ready. Eager.

Hands around my waist, he picked me up and walked through the shadowy parking lot. Headlights zoomed past. Horns blared in the distance.

The oppressive, humid heat settled in my gut, fed by his mouth on mine, increased by his calloused thumbs edging beneath my top, scraping across my breasts. And lingering over my nipples.

He came to a halt and put me down next to a sparkling crew-cab pickup. "Wow," I gasped when he released my breasts, wishing he hadn't stopped—the hard kisses or the nipple caresses. "Nicer than your work truck."

"Yeah. Thanks. You got condoms?" he asked, digging for his keys. "Did you come prepared?"

I thought of the three packets tucked in my back pocket. "Several."

He opened the rear door. I clambered inside and he climbed in after me. My lungs heaved, inhaling the scents of new car and arousal. My own.

The bench seat was plush; the truck hot. I was on fire.

"Good girl. I did too." He arched over the seat and started the engine. The big diesel rumbled to life and he flipped the a/c on high.

Returning to the backseat, Travis leaned against the opposite corner and stared at me in the neon light coming in through the windshield, compliments of the blinking *Electric Ed's* sign overhead.

When he exhaled long and loud, his breath rasped past my ears and settled deep in my belly as though he were five inches away instead of five feet. "Seems the sex kitten is more of a wildcat. You sure you want this?"

No guts... "Definitely."

"You a virgin?"

"Definitely not."

"Good. But I'd want you either way." Still sprawled in his corner, he struggled to untuck his shirt and open his jeans. "Will you...?"

In the shadows, I knelt on the seat beside him and zeroed in on his groin. Moving aside his shirttail with the back of my hand, I grasped his erection and bent over, bringing my face to his lap. Would he be able to tell I hadn't done *this* before?

"Lick me," he voiced the soft command with a hard edge, tearing through the buttons on his shirt to drape it on either side of his waist. "Ply that pretty pink tongue up and down my cock and don't stop 'til I tell you."

Heeding his instruction, I placed my lips against the solid, heated flesh and kissed upward from the base, along his shaft, to the wide head at the top. He knotted several fingers in my hair and guided me.

His other hand slipped beneath my jeans, fingers snagging on my satin panties as he teased along the crack of my ass and my body responded, flooding with arousal. Even though I could hardly focus on anything beyond what his hands were doing against my scalp and between my butt cheeks, I wrenched my attention from the desperate desire his actions wrought forth and focused on *my* actions. On what I could wring from him...

Dipping my head, I parted my lips and eased past his crown, tightening my hold on the shaft and sinking down, a measured draw of my mouth that took him deep inside. Once I'd gone as far as I comfortably could, I kept my lips snug and pulled upward. As his erection withdrew, my tongue eagerly swiped back and forth, exploring the new tastes, the new textures. A couple more advances and retreats and soon his hips were arching off the seat, pushing more of his rod past my lips as his hand in my hair kept me in place, his willing prisoner. His wildcat. At the thought, my heart sped like a race car.

"Bite me."

"*What?*" I paused to ask but my tongue didn't want to go far, busy investigating the ridge beneath his crown.

"I like a little pain," Travis grunted as though my efforts, if not painful exactly, were at least keeping him on his toes. "Makes me feel alive."

A thrill shot through me. Fear or adrenaline? I kept hold of his cock but raised up to look at him. "Are you into really kinky stuff?"

"I'm into only what two people agree on. Are you gonna bite me?"

"Can I suck you more instead?"

He gave a low laugh. "Go for it, baby."

I did, returning to take him within my mouth, as deep as I could. My tongue curved around his shaft and I pulled hard, the muscles in my throat and neck working as my cheeks suctioned against his dick.

"Yeah, like that."

Feeling braver, I gently grated my teeth around

the thick muscle. He made a sound of approval and shifted his torso. Winding his fingers into my center belt loop, he tugged me closer. When I complied, shuffling forward on my knees, he released my jeans to edge his fingertips beneath my panties. Sliding his strong hand over my butt cheeks and past parts inflamed with lust and longing, he touched my soaked flesh, teased my slit.

I groaned, wanting to come, wanting to wait, confused, just *wanting*. Needing.

Gripping my hair harder than before, he pulled my head up, dislodging his erection. I sat back on my haunches, my breathing choppy. My lips felt swollen and tingly. My loins did too, so sensitized that every motion was excruciating yet tempered with excitement, with anticipation. I stared at him, wishing we were outside, in the daylight...wishing that I could see him better.

"Take off your jeans," he ordered, stretching his long legs on the seat on either side of mine.

I obeyed, doing this contorted standing-kneeling thing, one foot on the floorboard, the other propped on the seat, as—totally lacking in grace but making up for it with enthusiasm—I scrambled out of my boots and the sweat-dampened denim as fast as I could. Under his watchful, glittering-in-the-shadows gaze, I tore off my panties.

Practically naked. In the backseat of a truck. With a near stranger. *Take that!* I told my inner vixen...then I retrieved my jeans and riffled the back pocket for a condom.

"Second thoughts?"

His husky voice halted my actions—but only for a moment. Brandishing the foil packet like a winning lotto ticket, I shot him a grin and climbed over his outstretched legs, wedging one of mine between him and the seat while keeping my outside foot on the floor, until I was straddling him, the starched denim of his jeans abrading my inner thighs. "Are you kidding?" I plucked at the wrapper and muttered to myself, "Darn things didn't say they were childproof." Then to him, "Do these look like the actions of someone having second thoughts?"

Chuckling in a low, smoky way that melted my insides, Travis held me steady with his powerful, work-roughened hands on either of my thighs while he shimmied beneath me until his back reclined on the seat. As I felt him widening his knees and hunkering into place, he released me to snare the packet from my fumbling fingers. The neon sign had barely flashed twice before Travis rolled the rubber down his cock and into place.

"I wish I'd gotten ones that glowed in the dark," I complained, wanting to see his dick.

"Next time," he grunted, placing his hands firmly on my hips and bringing me forward, over his groin.

Every muscle in my body spasmed at the thought of a promised *next time*, at the thought of *now*. I hovered above his upraised erection.

"Come here, wildcat. I've been thinking about this for weeks." Fingers pressed into my flesh, he centered me over his cock. My thigh muscles shook from the strain of holding back. To anchor myself, I slid my hands beneath his open shirt and up the sides of his beautiful, sculpted torso. It might not be clearly visible now, but I'd stared at his chest enough to memorize every contour, every tattoo...

Tattoos. Ignoring the twinge I experienced from mine each time I moved my right arm—heck, each time I breathed—I stroked my palms up the supple flesh, over the wicked snake, the skull and the cross, until I reached the pliable spot where his neck curved into his shoulders. And that's where I stayed, gripping the hard, rounded muscles, digging my nails into his skin.

While I'd been in my own little world, touching and exploring the fabulous body beneath me, Travis had been doing a bit of erotic exploration of his own, rubbing the head of his erection up and down my slit. When he nudged it into place, past swollen folds that were so incredibly responsive to this man and his touch, my hips convulsed as though zapped by an electric shock.

"Relax. You're more than ready." His fingers tightened and he pulled me down against his groin, ramming high inside my walls.

I screamed. My inner muscles rippled around him, drawing him deeper. His hands went to my ass where he kneaded the cheeks of my bottom, pulling them apart and lunging higher.

I lowered fully against his chest and my lips praised his neck...his collarbone...their ultimate destination, I realized dimly, the sun tattoo that had so fascinated me. As I tongued the first brilliant ray, he slammed up into me again and my pelvis tilted, bringing my clit in contact with his curly pubic hair.

"Kiss me, wildcat," Travis groaned and sought my wandering lips. When I turned my head to meet his demand, he thrust his tongue inside my mouth and rubbed it along mine. His body arced off the seat, plundering my flesh, plowing into me, just as I'd fantasized.

The big truck rocked as we heaved into each other. Travis raked his nails up my ass and groped at the base of my spine. A second later the tie securing my halter top gave way and he stroked his hands up my vertebrae, stopping at my nape to work on the bow I'd fashioned there. Once the knot was freed, Travis tugged on the halter from the side, whisking the thin cotton past my breasts and tossing it away.

"That's better." Hands firm below my armpits, he lifted me a few inches. "Just what I wanted to taste next." Travis kissed his way down my chin, my chest... His lips latched on to one nipple and he sucked.

The action might have been simple but it evoked a complex response as every particle in me came alive. My hips rotated, grinding my core against his groin. I rode him, thinking of horses, thinking of meadows, thinking of running free, riding a stallion bareback, riding this sexy, tattooed landscaper who was playing stud to my vixen.

Without warning, his teeth clamped down, biting my nipple, and I cried out.

"Want me to stop?" he asked around my breast.

God, no! I arched against him, frantic, needing to climax.

He lunged higher, harder, and while his lower body hammered into mine, he licked a deliberate, delicate trail around my breast and straight up to my neck and beyond, where he took possession of my mouth once again. Clasping one arm low across my back, Travis splayed his fingers on my spine and crushed me to him.

His other hand returned to my ass, gave one buttock a light slap, and dove between my thighs. Where he proceeded to reach past his cock to tease my clit from behind.

The action was so raw, so unexpected, that I squealed and rode him with everything in me. Kissed him with all I had. He sucked my bottom lip into his mouth and tongued the sensitive flesh he'd exposed. The second he released me, I returned the favor, only once I had his lip between mine, I bit down, worried it with my teeth. Playfully at first then passionately, uncaring whether it hurt.

He growled. A sound of pure approval.

His fingers plucked and pruned my clit,

nurturing the tiny seed, making it harden, grow, until I felt my orgasm burst through me, watering his fingers, sucking at his dick like parched earth seeking rain.

A long, low squeal came from my throat and I freed his lip, my tongue instinctively surging alongside his. Travis hummed his pleasure, kissed me more ferociously, and shot his load. His cock jerked within my quivering muscles. He groaned again and his head fell back to the seat, mouth open as he loudly exhaled. "Damn. Just...damn."

Cool air washed over my backside. I sighed, trying to catch my breath. His fingers relinquished their post between my legs and skimmed up my back. He encountered the bandage and circled it lightly.

In between ragged breaths, he raised his head and kissed me, softly this time. A tribute of sorts, his mouth paying tender homage to mine. "Want to go out for dessert?"

"You mean..." I exhaled on a cloud, floating somewhere between happy and delirious. "Like a date?"

"Hell yeah, I mean like a date. And then I'm taking you home. We need to wash your new tiger and put some cream on it."

The neon *Electric Ed's* blinked off, leaving us in near darkness. My fingers traced over his deltoid. His open shirt partially hampered my efforts but I still wanted to know, "Why is the sun your favorite?"

"Nighttime confessions? Okay. I'll trade. When I was younger, I did a lot of shit I'm not proud of. The sun is a reminder—look for the positive. Silver linings, light at the end of the tunnel and all that. Your turn. Do you really think you're boring?"

"Not anymore." I kissed his jaw, raspy with sexy stubble. "Do you have any Hershey's syrup in your fridge?"

"Think so. Don't know how old it is." He shifted and withdrew, causing renewed tingles to dance through my crotch. "Why?"

"Can we skip dessert? Just go back to your place, get the chocolate syrup and, um, you can eat me for dessert?"

"Wildcat, you're on." He slapped my bare bottom. "Now get dressed."

I rubbed my legs over his long, muscular ones. "Do I have to?"

"Death by innocence. You're gutsier than I expected."

That made two of us. "Complaining?"

"Nope. On the contrary, I'm forecasting clear and sunny skies."

Thanks for reading *No Guts, No 'Gasms.* The idea of sex with a total stranger remains one of my favorite themes to write. Add in some muscles and tattoos, and I'm a happy girl. :)

If you have a chance to write a review, it's always appreciated. Reviews and word-of-mouth are wonderful things you can do for authors you enjoy.

I thought we were going Christmas tree shopping with my boyfriend's parents.

He had other ideas.

Sexy, snowy ideas sprinkled with enough sparks

to melt any protests I might've made. Making snow angels has never been so naughty.

2500 words • Short 'n' Super Steamy • Happy Ending

Available at: http://bit.ly/o-oh-christmas-tree

If you'd like to sample my Regency writing in a steamy short, here's *The Pirate's Pleasure.*

Fresh from rejecting yet another suitor (determined to resist Mama's pressure to accept *anyone*—"Please, dear, before you're so far on the shelf it topples!"), Lady Roberta convenes a weekly writing group comprised of her three closest friends. Their literary efforts soon evolve—or devolve, depending upon one's point of view—from composing insipid lines of poetry to more erotic endeavors.

4000 words • Complete Story • Subscriber exclusive

Meet the ladies and read *The Pirate's Pleasure* here: http://bit.ly/pirates-pleasure

Romantic and Steamy Contemporaries

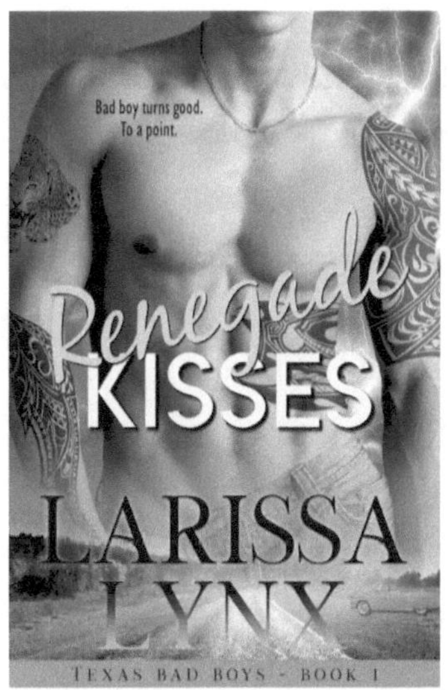

Renegade Kisses

Tattooed bad boy Nico faces his past, his doubts, and his demons to claim the woman who stole his heart.

If off-limits rich girl Alexis is champagne and hot yoga, then he's campouts and cold beer. They were perfect together—until *he* screwed everything up.

When he learns his "Sexy Lexi" is getting married tomorrow *to the wrong man*, Nico crashes her wedding rehearsal.

Before the night is through, he's gonna steal a kiss—and a whole lot more. He'll risk everything for the woman he loves, even if he has to kidnap her from the church to prove it.

Renegade Kisses is a full-length, stand-alone sexy romance with humor, emotion and a heartwarming Happily-Ever-After.

Available FREE from most vendors...

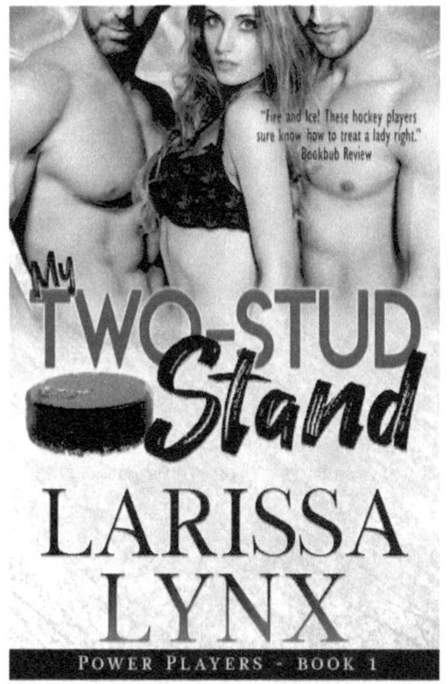

My Two-Stud Stand

Power Players Hockey Series, Book 1

Because sometimes, a girl just really needs a good, hard puck...

When a professional hockey player—Russian by birth, sexy by the grace of God—propositions me during my first and only foray into liberated sex with a stranger, I allow myself to be seduced with heavily accented words and devastating kisses, right up to Rurik's hotel room. Where his focused attentions quickly melt my natural inhibitions.

But then his roommate emerges fresh from the shower. Hold up—*two* men? I might have considered celebrating with one, *but both*?

Confronted with the prospect of a two-stud

stand, enraptured by Rurik's kisses and Jeff's speculative glower, I wage a debate with my protesting conscience. At stake? The night of my life. The prize? More orgasms than I know what to do with.

12,000 words • Reverse Harem • Sex with Strangers
*Available **FREE** from most vendors, grab **My Two-Stud Stand** now!*

Her Three Studs

Power Players Hockey Series, Book 2

Because sometimes, one puck just isn't enough...
I've just experienced my first one-night stand. With two studs! I can hardly believe it. Professional

hockey players Rurik and Jeff, whose caresses skated all over my body and brought it to life as no one ever has. But when the fun's over and I try to leave, they won't let me. Not alone.

Hiding out in the luxurious bathroom after the most spectacular sex of my life, I listen to the two men arguing over who will take me home. What's up with this? I'd been blazingly happy with my single night of sexy sin, never expecting anything more. No expectations means no chance for heartache, right? So why am I letting Jeff seduce me all over again? With kisses and conversations and promises of another night, another friend, the next time his team's in town...

Romantic 'n' Super Steamy • 52,000 words • Reverse Harem

A Heart for Adam...& Rick!

He promised me a treat.

A weekend on the lake—without the kids.

He didn't tell me he'd invited a friend.

6000 words • Reverse Harem • Short 'n' Steamy • Complete Story

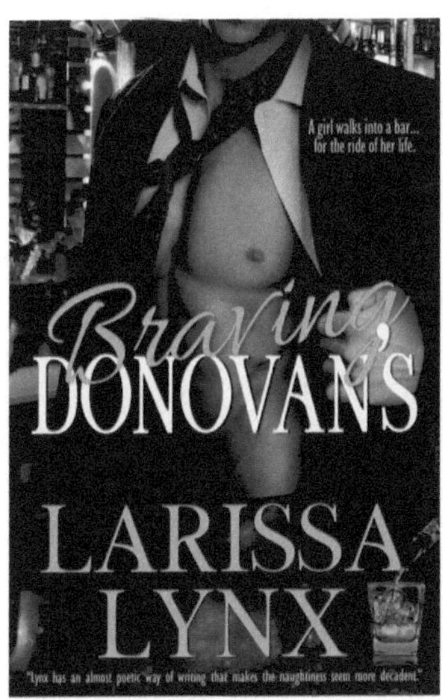

Braving Donovan's

A girl walks into a bar. Looking for some action.

That would be me—nervous but determined.

Wanting to do something brave and crazy, despite everything I've been taught to the contrary.

Actually, the bar's really a club, one that caters to fantasy fulfillment.

And I'm about to get in *way* over my head...

7000 words • Sex with Strangers • Fun ending • Complete Story

A lifelong Texan, Larissa writes sexy contemporaries and steamy regencies, blending heartfelt emotion with doses of laugh-out-loud humor. Her heroes are strong men with a weakness for the right woman.

Avoiding housework one word at a time (thanks in part to her super-helpful herd of cats >^..^<), Larissa adores brownies, James Bond, and her husband. She's been a clown, a tax analyst, and a pig castrator(!) but nothing satisfies quite like seeing the entertaining voices in her head come to life on the page.

Writing around some health challenges and computer limitations, it's a while between releases, but stick with her...she's working on the next one.

Learn more by visiting LarissaLynx.com.

www.ingramcontent.com/pod-product-compliance
Lightning Source LLC
Chambersburg PA
CBHW021149190726
48288CB00008B/2897